Barbara,

It was really nice
seeing you again. Sorry about
the title of the book (kinda tacky).
Hope to see you in the future.
Don't forget to use the
workable fixatur

Sincerely, Steve
Yenni

THE WONDERFUL LIPS OF THIBONG LINH

by Theodore Roscoe

THE WONDERFUL LIPS OF THIBONG LINH

by Theodore Roscoe

Illustrated by
Stephen Gervais

Donald Grant • Publisher
West Kingstown

1981

THE WONDERFUL LIPS OF THIBONG LINH

First Edition
ISBN 0-937986-36-4

Printed in the United States of America

ACKNOWLEDGMENTS

"On Account of a Woman" copyright 1936 by Popular Publications for *Adventure,* January 1936.
"The Voodoo Express" copyright 1931 by the Frank A. Munsey Co. for *Argosy,* October 10, 1931.
"The Wonderful Lips of Thibong Linh" copyright 1937 by the Frank A. Munsey Co., for *Argosy,* December 4, 1937.

CONTENTS

ILLUSTRATIONS

AUTHOR'S NOTE

Weird tales. Who doesn't like them? Since the days of Aesop they have fascinated mankind.

They have come in all shapes and sizes, composed of many ingredients. The scary. The eerie. The gory. The suspenseful. The occult. The grotesque. The supernatural. The monstrous. The baffling. The wizardish. The out-of-this-world. The inexplicable. In them, fantasy may blend with ghoulery or mysticism with murder to cool one's skin or prickle one's scalp.

Edgar Allan Poe was the early American star of first magnitude in this dark literary firmament. Although preceded by Washington Irving's immortal "Headless Horseman," Poe's procession of funereal weird tales had the nation happily shuddering for generations. A century of schoolboys delightedly devoured *The Masque of the Red Death, The Black Cat, The Cask of Amontillado, The Descent into the Maelstrom.* (One way of getting kids to read?) What adult could forget the ghastly climax of Poe's *Ligeia,* the horrors of *The Tell-Tale Heart,* the suspense in *The Pit and the Pendulum?* While *The Murders in the Rue Morgue* is usually classed as a detective-story classic, it may also be considered a weird. And do Poe's stories still exude a spine-chilling atmosphere? (Ask Vincent Price!)

Of course, British writers had long indulged the weird. Jonathan Swift's "Gulliver" delighted England in 1726 with a champion weirdo. Mary Shelley starred in the early British galaxy with *Frankenstein* casting long nightmare shadows in the candlelight of 1818. The later Gaslight Era shivered through a Hallowe'en of British weird tales — Stevenson's horror master-

9

piece, *Dr. Jekyll and Mr. Hyde,* followed directly by Mrs. Belloc Lowndes' Jack-the-Ripper shocker, *The Lodger,* to be succeeded in the 1890s by Bram Stoker's incomparable *Dracula.*

Nor were the French, Germans, Russians and Italians to be denied similar spine-chilling joys. Hugo's *Hunchback,* featuring the hideous *"Quasimodo"* among the gargoyles of Notre Dame, stands tall (though deformed) among the weird-tale greats. So do the grisly fairy stories recounted by Germany's extraordinary Brothers Grimm. Gogol in the Ukraine inspired contemporary readership chills. And for the young and old of Italy *Pinocchio* could be regarded as a weird morality tale.

In a more modern vein at century's turn fine specimens came from the imaginative inkwell of Ambrose Bierce, whose *Can Such Things Be?* remains a superb example of the fictional eerie. And from Henry James whose *Turn of the Screw* stands as a ghost story unrivalled in that eerie realm. Outstanding in a library of others was Algernon Blackwood, whose tales of the unexpected and uncanny cooled the blood in a day before air conditioning. Who could forget the prickle of such a book as *John Silence?*

Weird tales. They were fun to read. And it must be confessed by the present writer when aspiring to enter that story-telling field, fun to write. The three stories chosen by the present publisher, recognized weird-tale authority and *officianado,* Donald M. Grant, (who dredged them out of files in Little Rhody) are not presented with the pretension that they may measure up to the stellar classics in mention. They are offered in the hope they can at least make the grade as satellite specimens of the genre.

I would add they were written (as I assume were those by the past masters) with audience entertainment as the primary aim. True, in a number of the classic weird tales (e.g., *Black Cat* and *Dr. Jekyll)* a conscience angle or moral emerges. Virtue triumphs in many of the stories, or at least criminality and injustice are frustrated, or wickedness ultimately punished as when the stake is ultimately driven through Dracula's evil heart. Still, even in the older allegorical narratives, it would seem the masters never strayed from the objective of telling a compelling and entertaining story.

The present writer strove to follow that aim with the stories offered here. They espouse no cause. Peddle no propaganda. Preach no ideology. Nor expound some allegedly scholarly or important message. They were composed only as escapist fiction, designed to amuse. As would vaudeville turns endowed with no more significance than tap dancing, acrobatic stunting, barbershopping or Houdini magic.

However, although written nearly 50 years ago, these weird novelettes did show up with peculiarly current story angles. The first story's setting, Palestine, was originally used as a backdrop from a then seemingly remote geographic area involving Arab nomads and Old Testament lore. In 1930 the Dead Sea area remained as far off the front page as the Mountains of the Moon. Who could have guessed it would move so close to home in the late 1970s?

Similarly the Haiti setting — one visited by the author in 1931 — was far from that day's American fireside scene. Yet only yesterday a strange news item appeared in the Miami press reporting the current practice of Caribbean voodoo in that city, replete with the Haitian *obeah* witchcraft prevalent in the early '30s. And who back then would have supposed the fanatic cult described in my fiction story might foreshadow, as in a dark glass, the murderous cultist hysteria recently manifested in Jonestown?

By weird coincidence, too, the third tale is set in a once remote area known as French Indo-China, that tragically warscourged region headlined today as Cambodia and Vietnam. Who 50 years ago could have foretold the horrors to be visited on that verdant and innocent land?

Then if some of the features in my stories bear any similarity to peoples or situations existing today, the resemblances are by sheerest chance. If the characters or story lines happen to touch on sharp or controversial ideas here or there, such points, if any, were made only to develop fictional character, or forward action or illusion, or unfold the plot.

Again, these stories were written with audience entertainment in mind. Or, to put it another way, to satisfy the demands a well-known New York publisher once said he required of fiction — a narrative designed to maintain interest and keep the reader turning the pages.

It is this author's hope these weird tales, although written 50 years ago, will meet that exciting requisite, and keep the reader turning.

Theodore Roscoe
Ormond Beach, Florida, and
Block Island, Rhode Island
March 1980

ON ACCOUNT

OF A WOMAN

by

Theodore Roscoe

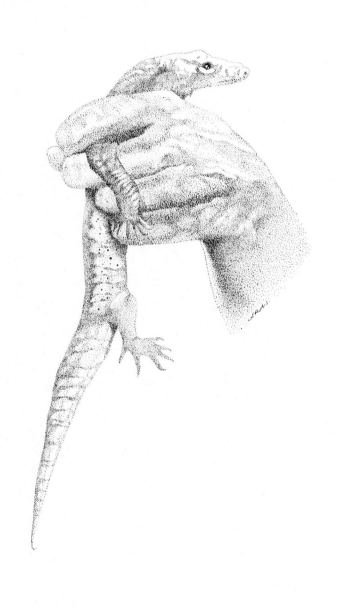

ON ACCOUNT OF A WOMAN

The ship, Cairo-bound, was steaming out of the Red Sea into the Gulf of Suez, and a sunset with more glory than all the battle flags of the world had transmuted an eastern shoreline to a coast of solid gold.

Farraday, the foremost animal collector in the business, had been moody, almost nervous throughout the afternoon. Ordinarily occupied with his specimen cages on the foredeck, he had paced in offish solitude behind the steering-engine house, gravity in his weathered angular face, eyes brooding on the passing shore. And at dinner, that night when the naturalist started his first spoonful of consommé, then flung napkin to lips, pushed back from the table and stalked from the saloon as if ill, his traveling companion, Mendel the metallurgist, was worried.

"What's the matter?" he wanted to know, coming abreast with the naturalist, who was hurrying aft. "You looked, when you started your soup, as if you'd been poisoned."

"I have." Farraday touched his forehead with a handkerchief. "That chef must have gone insane. That stuff tasted deadly to me. Deadly as — as sin."

Mendel suggested summoning the captain, but the naturalist shook his head.

"Not that way," he demurred. "That isn't what I mean."

When they stood by the jackstaff where the frigate birds wheeled, the metallurgist voiced some exasperation.

"Look here, Farraday, what's been eating you? All afternoon you've gloomed around by yourself, watching that Sinai coastline as cryptic as an Egyptian cat, and now a spoonful of soup sets you off as if a ghost had seen you. If there's anything I can do — "

"You started it," the naturalist said somberly. "Remember when our ship came in sight of Sinai? I said we must be passing over the spot where Moses led the Children of Israel across the Red Sea. The place where the waves rolled back to let the Chosen People cross dry-shod and escape the armies of Pharoah. You said you didn't believe in those Bible stories."

"I said I didn't believe in miracles," the metallurgist snapped. "Moses might have led his crowd across the Red Sea at some shallow spot that has since been dredged out by the Suez Canal engineers. Perhaps some conjunction of wind and tide drove the waters back. But there wasn't any so-called miracle. And I expressed surprise at you, a scientist, talking as if you believed there was. And what's this to do with a dish of soup?"

Farraday's eyes were focused on the tenuous gold thread that was land in the east; his voice came curiously solemnized from his lean and hardened jaws. "Coincidence, that's all. You disputing the miracles, then that soup. Miracles? There's the land they came from, that Near East littoral out there. As for Moses and his Children — I knew one of those Israelites. A woman with all the mystery of midnight and the wonder of day, a face and figure of pure magic, an allure and bafflement that could turn men into fanatics and set two friends clawing at each other like murderers."

The naturalist scrubbed his lips with his handkerchief as if to scour them of the memory; and the metallurgist, who had known him as a confirmed bachelor, regarded Farraday in mounting astonishment.

"Go inland," the naturalist pointed, "through those hills beyond Sinai and you'll come to the Gulf of Akaba. Arabia lies across the Gulf, and just north of the Arabian border you'll come to a place I don't like to think about. That's where I met this woman. I didn't believe in miracles, myself, in those days. Neither did a friend of mine who was with me when I met her. She had the sort of face that wouldn't believe in miracles, either. Bold. Hard. Wait till I tell you how hard. My friend pronounced her a woman who would take a dare, just the precious type of woman he wanted. He wanted her and I wanted her, and we almost murdered each other in cold blood to get her. Only a miracle saved us. Do you want to know what kind of poison was in my soup, tonight? Do you want to hear about this wonderful woman and the miracle that happened?"

Fixed on that flaming eastern shoreline, Farraday's eyes were dark with a light not reflected from the Red Sea sundown.

The metallurgist said he wanted to know.

The metallurgist was hungry when his friend began the story, but when it was finished he had lost his appetite.

Two years after the War (Farraday began) the natural history society I was working with decided to send me into the Arabian desert after specimens — a rare type of basilisk lizard, to be exact — and I was to go in from the Gulf of Akaba, work across the north end of Arabia and swing back south to the coast of the Red Sea. Egypt, Palestine and Arabia all meet at the Gulf up there, but they don't shake hands.

It's a foul neck of the woods at best, and two years after the World War wasn't best. Allenby's army had been around there, so had Lawrence. You'll recall the British made a lot of promises to the Arabs that London didn't keep, and some of the tribes didn't care if the War was over or not. If I wanted to get out of there with lizard skins — not to mention my own — I'd have to walk on eggs. My employers instructed me to sing low when I met any Arabs; then they sent me Rallston as my assistant collector!

It was a ticklish enough assignment without the extra hazard of this Johnny Rallston. A naturalist runs across some pretty wild specimens in his work, but Rallston was just about the wildest young mammal I'd been associated with. Indigenous to Australia, he hailed from Brisbane, and when I say "hail" I mean he came shouting, jaw out, fists cocked ready to go.

His father was a revivalist clergyman of the old hell's fire and damnation school, and the boy had been reared in a parsonage on prunes and proverbs — and a horsewhip, too, I fancy —

by the sort of maiden aunts who still wore bustles on the back of
their minds. Then the war had let him out of his cage and he'd
started off to see the world with Allenby. He'd been everything
from air pilot to cameleer, and after the Armistice he'd bummed
around the Near East on all manner of crazy jobs, finally landing a position with my outfit.

I'll never forget my first view of Rallston. He'd been with
the Society about a month, and he came slamming into our Cairo
office as if he owned the affair. He wore a British officer's cap,
insignia removed, set challengingly forward on a thatch of
bleached hair; a cowboy's grin in a face as ruddy as a cherub's;
impudence in green-blue eyes; a pair of whipcord riding
breeches that had lost their whip and most of the cord. Over his
shoulder he carried an expensive photographer's kit — "borrowed" from the department of signals — and his feet were bare.

"Sold the field boots," he told me with a grin. "Thomas of
London and worth most a ticket anywhere. Sold 'em to buy this
naval officer's wife a bit of jade. All I wanted was one dance because she was beautiful. She took the jade; then she wouldn't
dance with me 'cause I'm barefoot."

"Sold your boots to buy a trinket?" I gaped at Rallston.
"I thought you were working to save money and go back to
Australia?"

"Go home?" he laughed. "Not me! Not back to that parsonage. You never knew my old man. Believes every word of the
Bible, that sort of thing. Say, he almost had me studying for the
ministry."

"And why didn't you?"

"I couldn't believe," he told me, "in miracles."

We came to be fast friends the following months in Cairo,
and I thought I knew Rallston pretty well. I was fifteen years
younger, myself, in those days, and we got in some wild scrapes
together around the town. I didn't know what was the matter
with him, but I thought I could guess. Typical minister's son
breaking loose from too much early repression. Out to paint
the town red. His hatred of that home parsonage and all it rep-

resented amounted to a phobia. He read all the sophisticated agnostic literature he could lay his hands on, and called himself an atheist.

"I've chucked all that religion stuff," he liked to say. "Old-fashioned bunk, that's all it is. I've got a new ideal."

Apparently this new ideal had nothing to do with keeping solvent or sober, but he did his work well enough and the Society kept him on. He had a likely fist, and he knew the Arab lingo. That's why they sent him on the Arabian lizard-hunting expedition to be my assistant.

Now you may think yourself acquainted with a chap around the city, but you never know a man until you're off with him in some isolated spot like that jumping-off Gulf of Akaba place, north end of the Red Sea. That's where I first came to know the real matter with my Australian assistant collector. That's where I learned about his "new ideal." Rallston was a collector, all right, but not of lizards. I collected lizards. Rallston collected women!

Women, women, women! That boy had gone girl-crazy. Let a British pleasure yacht come steaming up the coast and there was Rallston swimming out to the ship — quite literally — with a rose in his teeth. Let a caravan come grunting and snuffing over the sand dunes, and Rallston was down in the oasis to meet it, like as not fighting three beachcombers for the hand of some desert belle before the camels had time to kneel. I thought when we got clear of the seaport that marked our base of supplies, and started into the desert, he'd get over it, but the desert was worse.

Do you know why he lugged that photographer's outfit with him? To take pictures of beautiful women, that was why. To photograph the lovely ladies he always thought he was meeting. His tunic pockets were stuffed with snapshots. Egyptian dancing girls in seven veils. Moslem debutantes with one eye wistful behind bars. Circassian "princesses" in fantastic costumes from heaven knew where.

Officers' wives. Russian refugees. All the backwash the War had left stranded on the Near East beach and rarer specimens from the direction of Mecca. Daytimes I'd be off bottling basilisks, Rallston would be camera-hunting ladies off in oasis palms. Nights he'd lie sprawled on the sand, sorting through his precious photographs and sighing like a crack-brained Romeo.

Like a lot of sophisticated young men who went through the war and came out thinking they were tough, this Australian hellion was as sloppily romantic inside as a bouquet of sweet peas. Having coughed up an overdose of religion, he had proceeded to swallow in its stead — on an empty stomach — such a mess of romanticism as would have sickened St. Valentine.

"Tagging around after every skirt you see," I gibed him one night. "You're too smart to believe the Old Testament, but fall for every female who gives you the eye. Keep up this game, and you'll go home sooner than you think. In a box."

For the first time Rallston's eyes were sober. "I won't go home in a box or any way. Not till I've found that ideal."

"And what's this wonderful ideal?" I had to jeer.

"None of 'em have come up to it so far," he admitted seriously, "but I'm going to find a woman, my lad, that's something a bit different from the Alice-sit-by-the-fires you've got back in civilization. No more clinging vines for me. I don't want citified swank and lipstick either. I want a woman with spirit, a woman" — he swept his arm in a Shakespearean gesture — "who isn't all tied up with corsets and rules of conduct and religion. She's got to be gorgeous looking and all, but she's got to be something more. That's why I like the girls in this country around here. No knitting and rocking chairs and chaperoned tea-parties in this neck of the woods. They have to fight their way to get around. They won't take no for an answer. That's what I want, old man. The sort of women the only thing she *will* take is dare. Righto! A woman who could give or take a dare."

So that was the ideal my assistant collector had substituted for his old-time religion. That was the reason for his battling from one bar-room to the next and his midnight excursions where angels feared to tread. I saw what he meant, all right. Clumsily phrased, but the mental picture he conveyed was a back-to-nature dream girl riding a white horse across wind-

swept horizons, beautiful as Godiva, spritely as Eve and bold as Ninon de Lenclos with a whip.

And of course he was looking through just the region where you'd never find such a girl. Wind-swept, starry-eyed and nature-free as an Arab's daughter may look as she rides across the dunes, your desert maiden is most hide-bound and rule-booked of all the breed. Allah to her is a great big thunder-cloud waiting to pounce; Life is one long inhibition and next to that she's scared of her henna-whiskered menfolk. And the next biggest sin in a Moslem maiden's category is to let some white unbeliever snap her photograph.

I told you there was trouble enough to begin with, and now you've got the set-up on my assistant collector, Rallston. I scarcely have to tell you how the storm broke. Lord knows, I'd warned him. But advising your fellow man about women — especially if you've knocked around together and happen to be nearly of an age — is something you can't do. I was fool enough, myself, on that score, and nobody to preach. You'll see I didn't hold any monopoly on the brains.

I was bottling basilisks in my tent on the sands one evening when Rallston came walloping over the horizon as if the devil were after him. Dust trailed like the smoke from an express train behind his racing camel, and not one devil, but twenty were after him. Twenty Arab horsemen bunched together, cloaks bannering, yells yapping from their beards and bullets snapping from their guns.

"Run!" Rallston shouted at me. "Run! They'll kill you!"

I had just about time to saddle my *mehari*, and that was all. Water casks, rifles, rations, baggage, collector's equipment, everything had to be left behind. It was touch and go with those desert nomads shooting the callouses off my camel's heels; our only chance lay in outdistancing those ponies to the Red Sea coast and we were a good many miles up the north end of Arabia from the Red Sea.

Darkness swept down out of Asia and the desert was blotted by India ink. There wasn't a star in that blackness, or a moon. I think there was an upper layer of sand blowing overhead, and the firmament was blanked out. A wonderful situation when your compass was miles behind.

By midnight we were lost, and by sunrise we might have gone over the edge Columbus' sailors were afraid of, deep in a wilderness of canyons and barren mountain ranges ablaze in the sun like hills of scrap iron. The Red Sea was nowhere in sight, but our pursuers were. They kept right on chasing us, deeper and deeper into those burning hills of rock, and they never gave up until late afternoon.

Rallston and I pulled our doddering camels into the shadow of a big yellow boulder, and watched our enemy go. They fired a few discharges into the air as a final warning, turned their horses and rode back over a ridge, vanishing in the dust-haze toward Arabia. Rallston lounged against the rock and watched the departure with a rueful grin.

"By Jove, that was a shave! Imagine them going off the deep end like that, just because I was taking this Arab girl's picture." He patted the camera-box slung at his side, and the corners of his mouth went down. "She wasn't worth it, though. Just like all the rest. Didn't care when I held her hand, but screamed when I snapped the camera. That brought her old man and all those devils down on me like a pack of mad dogs — "

I wanted to come down on him like a pack of mad dogs, myself. All night and all morning of that crazy race I'd been too mad to speak. Now when I blew up my tongue was so swollen with thirst I could only stand croaking and waving a fist at the sky.

"You've done it this time, you crack-brained fool! You realize we're lost? Lost! My Mauser rifles, my Zeiss binoculars, maps, five hundred dollars worth of collector's equipment, eight weeks work picking up specimens — "

"Honest, buddy, when I get the money I'll pay you back."

"Eight weeks work, specimens, probably my job, every-thing — " I shook my fist at the horizon where the Arabs had vanished — "everything lost back there in those sand dunes, just because you wouldn't keep your girl-crazy hands off the first female who smiled at — "

"She wasn't smiling," he corrected me, "she was crying. Standing in that oasis with her hands over her face. I thought she was swell when I first saw her. She was wearing these little ankle bells — "

"Ankle bells!" I panted. "I don't care if she was wearing the bells of Saint Mary's. Get it through your head that we've run off the map and we haven't any water! Not a drop! Only a miracle got us out of that," I raged; then I flung an arm at the landscape around us. "It'll take another miracle to get us out of this!"

"Bah!" Rallston snapped. "You know I don't believe in such rot. I'd hate to depend on Bible magic to get out of anything. I got you into this, and I'll get you out of it."

He was a cool one, all right, and scanning the gray cliffs around us, I would not have expected divine intervention, myself. There are some places on the globe where faith can waver, and that was one of them. Now that I had a chance to look at where we were, I wasn't sure we were on the globe. You've seen pictures of Death Valley. Well, this was Death Valley doubled. Even the air was dead. Heat rained down through a silence as quiet as deafness, and the rocks lay around on shelves of pumice and limestone like white bones.

There wasn't a breath of air or a jackal as far as the eye could see. Great fissures had cracked the floor of the valley we were in, and the canyon walls sheared up as silent and bare as deserted skyscrapers. Ashes. That's what the landscape made me think of. Dead ashes. Westward where the sun was lowering, as if in a hurry to withdraw its blood-stained eye from this scene of desolation, a range of cliffs stood up jagged as the roofline of a shelled town. I tell you, there wasn't a single sign of life.

I'd never seen a place like that on the Arabian map. Maybe we'd ended up among the craters on the other side of the moon. It was a hell of a country. I could smell the sulphur.

"All because of this damned dream girl of yours," I sneered at Rallston. "Well, what are you going to do about it? The camels

had a good feed yesterday afternoon and they can keep going. But we'll be dead and cured as figs by tomorrow afternoon if we don't find water."

He pointed west up the valley.

"The Red Sea ought to be over there. I'll ride that way, and you take it east. We'll meet back at this big rock at sunset. Okay?"

I told him I wouldn't die of grief if I never saw him again, and we set out in opposite directions looking for water. But the moment Rallston's featherbrained head was out of sight I was sorry. There was something about the burning silence of that gray landscape that got up under my skin the minute he was gone.

I started leading my camel, and my boots sent echoes up the canyon, echoes that died of loneliness away up the cliffs against the sky. A kicked pebble would go rattling across the rocks with the disturbance of a rat in a tomb, and when I sat down on a boulder to rest, the silence flowed up around me in a pressure that hurt my ears.

A couple of miles by myself in that solidified, ten-million-ton hush, and I was suffering for companionship as avidly as drink. Water was nowhere to be seen. Just calcined cliffs and emptiness. I might have been the first man along that fissured valley since the time of Exodus, and I felt pretty tiny among those skyscraper walls of stone.

The queerest sensation stole over me, something quite apart from the nervousness of fatigue or fright. A feeling of evil cloaking this burned-out landscape. A sort of repugnance mixed with fear, if you can imagine the feeling. The sort of shudder you might experience on passing a leper island far at sea, or standing before an empty house with the blinds drawn on an evil street. There was something about that scorching emptiness of stone that was bad.

The oddest panic came over me. I wanted to run. I wanted to make a lot of noise and get out of there. I could see why those outraged desert tribesmen hadn't followed us in these hills. I could have throttled Rallston for losing me in this landscape, but I give you my word, when sunset started slanting ochred shadows across the rocks, I mounted and rode back to our rendezvous as if the legions of Eblis were on my track.

Just as I reached the big yellow boulder, there was Rallston riding out of the west the same way. A second his camel was silhouetted atop that ragged ridge with red sky between its legs; then he came on the gallop, riding the hump like a jockey, hair wild, camera flying on its strap, larruping along the valley bottom as if to outstrip the long gray shadows that were reaching like giant fingers after him.

I was mighty glad to see him coming, that's the truth. But when I saw his face my heart contracted with fresh alarm. Plastered with white dust from boot to crown, he looked like a wild-eyed ghost scared to grinning, until he came close enough for me to see his eyes, bloodshot not with fear but excitement. Before I could muster a yell, he was off his camel with a rodeo rider's leap, bounding at me through the dust-whirl.

"I've got her!" he screamed at me. "By God, Farraday, I've got her!"

"Water!" I cried.

"The woman, you fool!" Rallston laughed and capered around me like a crazy man, holding up his precious photographer's kit. "The woman I've been looking for. Beautiful! Marvelous! Best looking woman you ever saw, and she's got more nerve in her little finger than you ever heard of. A pack of Arabs are holding her captive in a village the other side of those cliffs," he screeched at me, "and we're going back to rescue her tonight!"

Word of honor, I could have killed him there and then. Shot him down in cold blood. That crack-potted, romance-crazy Romeo! Send him after water in this thirst-smothered wilderness and have him come back blabbing out a love story. I don't know what did stop me from killing him, except that you just can't kill fellows of Rallston's kidney. He had that hell-for-leather, sword-and-cloak, cow-jump-over-the-moon quality which charmed the lives of Casanova and Cellini and all those

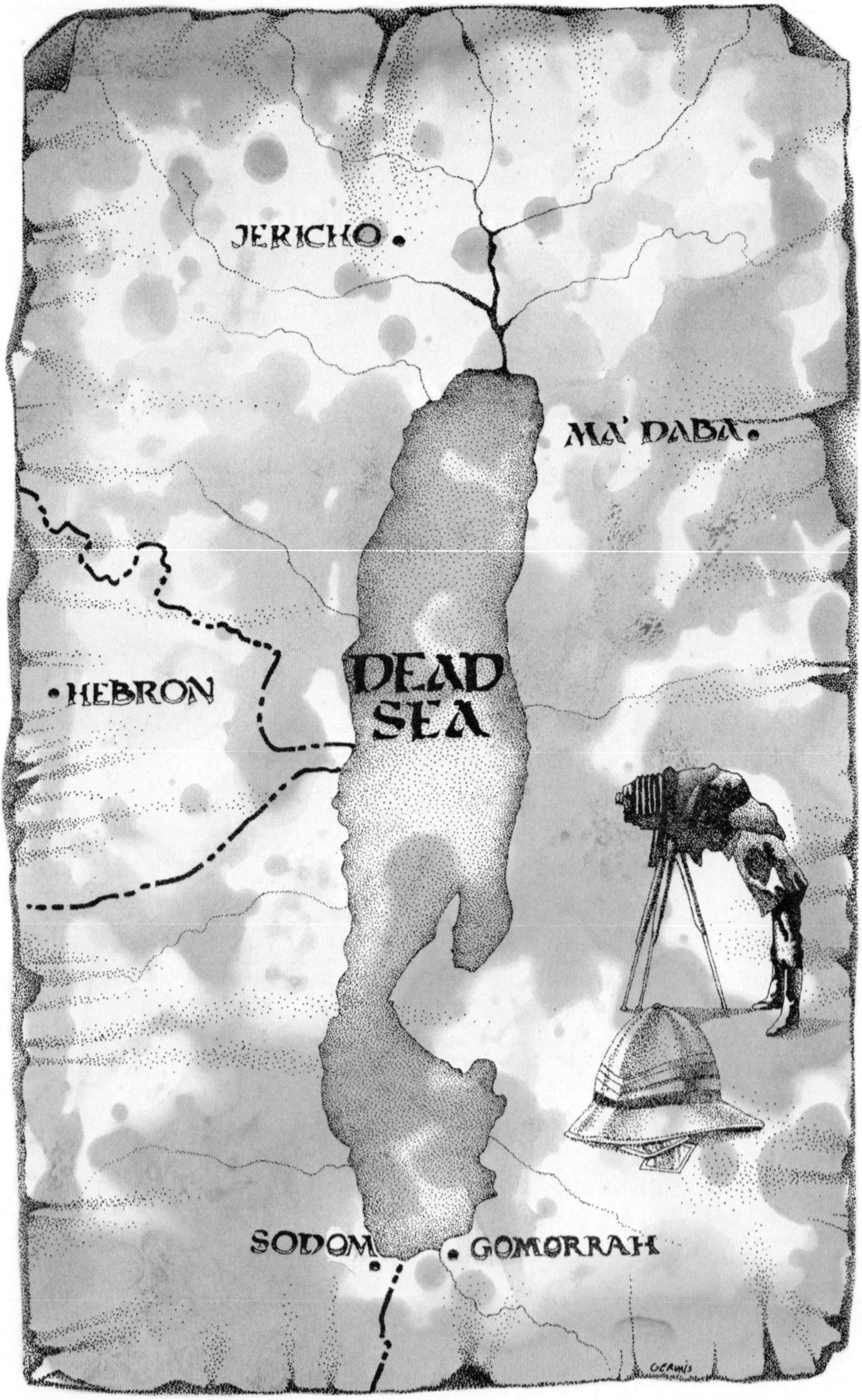
JERICHO
MA'DABA
DEAD SEA
HEBRON
SODOM
GOMORRAH

scapegrace matinee idols who balcony-climbed their way through history and got away with it.

Those velvet-panted rapscallions were salesmen, that's why. They talked their way into it and turned around and talked their way out of it. But they were tongue-tied bumpkins compared to my assistant collector Rallston selling me his latest heart-throb in that gray valley of petrified desolation, that night.

"Rallston," I snarled at him, "I'm going to knock your damned lovesick block off for this. Instead of asking for water in that village you were playing post office with some dame. Before I go over there to get a drink I'm going to break your head."

"Like hell," he countered, waving his arms. "You're going to help me save this woman, see? She's not like them, Farraday. She's not an Arab!"

He knew that angle would break down my sales resistance, and once he got his teeth in that opening, he didn't let go. He outshouted me, and I began to listen. It was all pretty queer against that Valley of Death background with Rallston's voice petering out in microscopic echoes up the cliffs. If I'd had any sense I'd have whacked that Australian on the jaw right at the start, but I've said I didn't hold any monopoly on the brains, and you'll see.

When I'd left him that afternoon, Rallston had scouted over that western rim of cliffs sniffing for water, and no sooner topped the rise than he'd found it. Unfortunately it wasn't drinking water, though. As far as Rallston could tell, the water beyond those cliffs was the Red Sea.

"A devilish barren coast," he told me, "with a smell in the air. Alkaline. There's a yellow fog combing in from the western horizon, and all I could see was a couple of small boats way out. A shoulder of mountain stretched seaward under the cliffs; from where I was I couldn't see the other side of that headland, but it sure is a desolate spot. I hiked my camel down to the shore thinking I'd start around the headland, hoping to find a town."

Rallston's hopes were raised by finding a bumboat in a sort

of rocky lagoon, a good-sized sailing barge about the build of a big launch with a forward hold for stowing freight.

"There's still oars in the row-locks and a deckboom with block and tackle unlimbered, like someone's put in to pick up cargo. But when I get near enough, I see that hull's been there a long time. Beached a couple of years. Sail gone to rag. The forward hold's empty, and so's a water cask under the rowing thwart. That dry keg and a skull lying up the beach told me what happened. Somebody'd come ashore and started afoot around land's end. Died of thirst and never been found. It's got my wind up a bit, that skull."

It got my own wind up, hearing Rallston tell about it.

"What's this deserted native bumboat and a skull got to do with your dream girl?" I wanted to know. Rallston was reciting this detail with all the wordage of a newspaper broadcast, and I yearned to hear the end of it and wring his neck.

"I'm coming to that," he panted. "I'm coming to that. I'm telling about the boat because we're going to use it for the rescue. I'm sure that Arab village doesn't know it's there. Well, I started my camel around this headland, taking the same path that skull had been following. About two miles up over the headland, there's the town on the other side."

He halted to draw maps in the dust with his boot-toe.

"The beach spreads out under cliffs too steep for an eagle, see? There's a batch of native boats along the beach, and the town's hugged against the base of the cliffs like a bunch of white blocks piled there by high tide. It's a Moslem stronghold, judging by the minarets, a hell of a tough-looking town."

Having reason to fear the Arab temper, my assistant hadn't started down hot-foot to beg for water, but had tethered his camel and climbed down through the rocks to spy. At first he thought the village was deserted; then he saw the whole population, like a crowd of sheeted ghosts, massed on the beach under the headland. Right under the rock where he was crouching.

"And that's where I saw *her!*" Rallston shook me by the arms. "She was standing in the middle of that ragged, stinking

swarm, the dust standing up around her like smoke. The whole crowd was hooting, yelling, hollering around her in some kind of dance, and dragging her — *dragging* her, you hear me? She was chained, Farraday! Chained by the ankles to a flat platform of planks that was hitched to a camel. That gang of Arab wolves was dragging her down the beach. You think she was crying out, fainting? She was not! She was standing upright like a soldier, Farraday. A white mantle pulled tight around her and the sort of figure — say, when I think of those heathens screaming at her, it makes me sick!"

In the sooty gloaming that had filled the valley about us, Rallston's eyes were glittering like a cat's. He made me see that woman and the Arab mob pulling her down the beach. He walked up and down, clenching and unclenching his fists as his voice painted the picture. He dug his father's best sermon-tones out of his memory to preach me the story of that woman's figure and how the Arabs dragged her and mobbed around her.

"And she's beautiful," Rallston shook me. "Young. Beautiful. Stood there, ankles chained to that platform, and never made a sound nor shivered a finger. Even when she saw me up there in the rocks she never made a sound. Get this! She saw me there. Looked straight at me. Her head was turned on her shoulder all the time, disdainful, and when the drag went under the rock-shelf where I was, she looked right into my face. Did she scream for help? Not her! Any other woman would have screamed and given me away. This girl stood steady as Gibraltar. Didn't move a muscle. I couldn't see her eyes for the shadow, but her face was proud as a queen's, not a sign of fear. Head to her little bare feet she was simply covered with that stinging white dust, but her chin was up, I tell you. Her mouth. Defiant. Damn near contemptuous. Of the mob and — and me, too. 'Come and get me,' she looked at me with that expression. By God! like a challenge. 'Come and get me if you're big enough. I don't think you can do it, but come and get me if you think you're big enough. I dare you!' "

Rallston's lips went white at this part of his story, and the sweat beads glittered like mercury on his knotted forehead. I could feel my own pulse getting up speed. Talk about Latins — it takes the Anglo-Saxon to play the heroics. Already I'd forgotten my lips were splitting from thirst.

"What happened then?" I whispered. "What did they do with her then?"

"Then the whole rotten hubbub went off down the beach," Rallston cursed, "and she just kept looking back over her shoulder, chin raised, looking up at me with that expression. I couldn't help her. All I could do was lie low and watch. watch that mob of brutes drag her to a hole in the rocks down the headland, a little cave. They left her there. Posted a dirty beggar with a big iron spear on guard, and streamed back to their filthy village. She was looking back at the last. My God, for all I know they're going to kill her. You've got to help me save her, Farraday! I'm going back and get her out of there tonight if it's the last thing I live to do!"

I said harshly:

"It'll be the last thing you'll live to do, all right. Listen, you fool. How can two of us attack an Arab village tonight or any night? Croaking for water, unarmed — "

"We'll surprise them," he blazed at me. "That cave isn't far from the water and the town's about a mile up the beach, away from the headland. We'll row around the headland in the dark, take her on the rush!"

"Take her where?" I swore. I was weakening, and it made me mad. Where could you take a woman in that desert of stones? Even the atmosphere was petrified.

Rallston swung an impatient arm.

"Take her to sea, man! To sea! There's a fog out there. We wouldn't have a chance going inland, but they'll never see us in that fog. All we've got to do is make the ship lane to Suez and we'll be picked up by midnight. Look!"

Now how do you suppose that lad ended his sale's talk? He was a devil of a boy, all right. He began to tear into his photographer's kit; dumped out his camera, rolls of film, little bottles

of chemical, all the truck these vagabond photographers around
fairs and boardwalks have to carry. Next thing I knew, he'd
fished from an envelope, a damp, glazed picture. A photograph,
on my word!

"I got her," he panted through his teeth, "just as the mob
was dragging her away. Snapped the camera just at the second.
Too much dust and no time to focus; then I had to stop and develop the thing in twilight up in those cliffs and only a little
water from my bottle in my kit."

A little water in his kit and he'd used it for photography!
But I never thought about it then. I was staring at that photograph and that photograph was staring at me. There wasn't much
light left to see it by, but there was enough. Enough to see the
white figure of a woman standing on a wooden drag in the midst
of a hooded, dark-whiskered mob; her mantle pulled tight about
her, her back to the camera, face turned on her shoulder, chin
lifted above the coiling dust.

Some women can hug a woolen wrap around them and
make it sheer as a veil. Only it wasn't the figure that bothered
me. It was the expression on the woman's face. Rallston hadn't
missed it when he called it, "Come and get me. I dare you!" But
he hadn't gone far enough. All the defiance and scorn of a
woman for the terrors of a man's world were in that expression.

Maybe she was in trouble, but she'd ask nobody's advice.
There was independence in that chin, neither fear nor humility.
It was a beautiful face, wilfully beautiful — the face of a lost *Peri*
who defied the devils and taunted the angels to the rescue. The
challenge and beauty of that face struck up out of the photograph, dim as it was, and made my senses swim.

"Maybe they're going to kill her," Rallston hoarsed out.
"Or they're holding her for ransom! Are you going to leave her
chained in that cave for the hands of those brutes?"

"Rallston," I cried, "what are we waiting for?"

Did you think there was a woman so wonderfully bold and
beautiful just the sight of her photograph would bring you
running? Well, you don't know the half of how wonderful that

woman was! Rallston jumped his camel and I grabbed mine and followed him up the valley and over the western cliffs with no more thought of the danger than the proverbial fool in a place forbidden to the angels. And there was none of the windy distance, no healthy oceanic sweep to that seascape.

A moon that looked moldy was sneaking down a low-hung sky as our camels topped the crags, and I got my first view of the sea. The beach far below was a ragged thread of lime. Rocks were mounded like slag along the shore, waste deposit left there from some long-ago reducing process, some overwhelming fire that had killed even the stones. The smell of that ancient fire was still in the night, sulphurous.

The water that had come too late had lain there too many centuries, yellowed, stagnated. Not far from the shoreline a saffron fog that might have been the smoke of that ancient, now-forgotten holocaust was banked up under the sky to blot the horizons.

Can you imagine a sea gone stale? Sweeping in with long undulant strides that came from no impulse in the earth but might have been started by the moon, the swells washed the coast with a sullen mutter that only undertoned the silence.

If I didn't like the hinterland we'd come from, I liked that coast even less. It couldn't be the Red Sea. The scrap iron cliffs, the clinker-like shore, the sea under the moon made me think of water in the firebox of a cast-off iron stove.

"Turn the camels loose here," Rallston ordered in a voice trembling with excitement. "There's the boat I told you about. Hurry."

That boat with its empty thwarts, its dried watercask, its sailcloth with the moon shining through, oars abandoned and that silent skull for a watcher up the beach, did nothing to cheer the scene. Surf creamed against the hull, booming a leaden echo through the square hatchway in the foredeck, the sound coming up from an empty cargo hold. Not unlike a small canal barge, the craft looked about as seaworthy as that Norsemen's gondola they found on the coast of Labrador.

But I couldn't back out now. My companion dredged a rusty anchor out of the shallows, and side by side on the thwart, each with an oar, we pulled our brains out to get her around the headland. Like a thieving galleon we thefted around land's end, and I was sweating like a teakettle when Rallstone steered us into a hideaway between tall rocks and told me we'd reached the spot.

Spot was right. The beach there curved like a gigantic simitar flat under the moon, and when I saw the white-walled village at the far end of its tip, I held my breath.

"There's the town," Rallston whispered. He was leading me through a goat-jump trail up the rocks, stooped over, tense, stealthy as an Indian. "And" — he stopped to fasten sinewy fingers around a loose rock — "there's the cave and the guard. Now!"

As Rallston gritted, "Now!" he sprang from the shadows like a panther. I had a momentary glimpse of a dark aperture scooped out under the cliff's overhand and a figure posed on the threshold, a ragged figure leaning on a spear. *Slug!* The man's turban muffled the blow. Rallston's rock dropped like a meteor and the Arab fell. My assistant collector collected the heavy iron spear, spun, beckoned, darted into the cave. I jumped in after him, stiffened as my boots hit over the threshold, stopped. Mr. Rallston had already stopped. Together we stood. And stared.

She was waiting in the inner darkness of that close-walled den, barefoot on her platform, her toes pointed toward the back wall, her head turned on her shoulder, face toward the door. Moonbeams poured yellow-green through the arch in the rocks and touched her curved, tense figure with gelid radiance, cold as witch-shine.

She was tall as a man, and from heels to crown in the dimness she sent off a white glow, ghostly as one summoned from the astral plane. Beneath the stiff folds of her tight-drawn shawl, her eyes stared in colorless, fixed immobility, stared at us in a way that put creeps through my hair.

Not a feature in that white face stirred. Not a muscle under the white-dusted cloak. Face posed in that over-the-shoulder "come get me if you think you're big enough" expression, she stood. Not a mouse of sound from her, and motionless as rock.

It was Rallston who fractured the silence, and when that rascally Australian opened his lips the whisper came out of them like a rush of air from a broken tire valve.

"Good God! Farraday! It's a *statue!*"

Well, I saw what had happened. That woman-daffy Australian's mind had been so stuffed with visions of his dream girl that, coming suddenly on a statue which met his romantic requirements, he'd failed to distinguish it from flesh and blood. There was always this wonder woman's picture in the cornea of his eye, and dust and a few shadows had tricked him. I started to give him a tongue-lashing. I was going to call him every name in the directory for bringing me across limbo to rescue an image. Then I stopped.

"I didn't know," Rallston was groaning. "I swear to God she looked real as life — "

Looked real as life? That statue *was* real as life. Rallston wasn't the only one who'd been tricked. The eye of his British military camera had been tricked, too. Anything that could deceive a lens made for penetrating camouflage had to be pretty lifelike, and I found myself staring at the sculptured woman's face in deepening astonishment.

Eye to eye with the thing, I couldn't drag my glance away. That sculpture had life to its very eyelids. Detail, chin, cheek, lips, a curl of hair on the forehead, texture of the shawl, the tight folds of the mantle outlining a lissom thigh, every detail had been carved to perfection.

How many statues have you known that could convey an expression? I'd been around the Louvre and I'd seen the Greeks. You'll suggest Praxiteles, and he was a master sculptor, but he never did anything as good as that woman in the cave. The figures in the Louvre were lumps of clay by comparison. This statue fairly breathed. Another moment and the lips would speak, demand us to take the chains off her ankles, be arrogant about it, too.

I couldn't tell whether she was marble or granite from the coating of dust, but whatever rock she was hewn from was vital in contrast to the burned-out slag of that wilderness. The thing came over me like a wave as I stared. Can you see the thoughts through my head? The first shock of astonishment followed by the second of awe?

I had to put out a finger, touch that stone to make sure. If genius shows in slavery to detail, if art means creating a veri-similtude to life, that statue had it. A master artist had done that piece of work. The greatest sculptor in the universe! It was a wonderful statue!

"It's wonderful!" I gasped at Rallstone. "Wonderful!"

His voice was low, throaty. "The woman I've been looking for all my life — a statue!"

"Don't be a fool," I whispered at him. "This is worth a thousand flesh-and-blood women! Why, its the greatest bit of carving in the world. To think these Arabs have kept it hidden in a cave. It must be over hundreds of years old, brought here by Arab pirates. But it isn't Athenian. That artist was long before Athens. Have you any idea what a thing like this is worth?"

I saw Rallston's lips had wried back in a grin. He was nodding, breathing hard.

"Come on, then. Let's get her out of here."

Looking back on that part of this story, I sometimes wonder if that atheistic minister's son hadn't put one over on me, after all. I sometimes wonder if he hadn't known it was a statue all along, hadn't pretended his bafflement and surprise. Guessing I'd never help him abduct any piece of statuary at the risk of my neck, he'd cooked up the woman angle, brought the snapshot to convince me because he needed my help in lifting the thing.

Well, he didn't have to convince me when I saw it, whether or no. I wanted that statue as I never wanted anything before,

GERVAIS

and so did Rallston. Any fool could have seen the genius in the thing. As to the lifting, both figuratively and actually, it was a job for two men.

Rallston attacked the chains fastening it to its platform, prying at the links with the spear, while I wrapped my arms around the statue and strove to shift its weight. Sweat broke on my forehead. The thing was heavier than three tombstones; must have weighed half a ton.

"Hold on," I puffed at Rallston. "We couldn't carry her out of here if there were six of us. We'll pull it on the drag!"

I sped a glance out of the cavern and up the beach to the walls of the moonlit town, expecting any second hell would pop. I didn't need any little bird to tell me what would happen if those Moslems discovered us pilfering their treasure. They knew the value of this statue, or they wouldn't have kept it hidden in a cave.

Then it occurred to me they might worship this wonder. Islam forbade idolatry, but there were tribes in Arabia who dated their customs to the days of Solomon and Sheba — if this image were a fetish and Rallston had spied it during some religious festival, there'd be triple hell if we were caught.

"Snap into it," Rallston goaded me breathlessly. "We've got to get out of here before that guard wakes up. Shove! Give her a shove!"

To this day I don't know how we ever budged that woman. The drag had no runners and we might have set out to move Mohammed's mountain. Teeth set, veins jutting, we put shoulders together and hands on the platform's end, braced our feet on the cave wall and pushed like the twins of Hercules. On the stone floor Rallston's boots skidded and thrashed like the drive-wheels of a freight engine trying to start on wet tracks.

We panted, puffed, swallowed oaths. Then for no reason at all the thing came unglued from its lethargy; platform and statue went slithering out into the moonlight past the upturned toes of the unconscious sentry. The platform gave a little scream as it scraped out over the stones, and for half an instant I thought the woman had come to life and voiced a cry.

My word, I did. I shook with anxiety, fearing the town would hear that screech, but the distant white walls went on sleeping, like the recumbent guard.

Rallston gave the guard a second crack on the head for good luck, and we started our wonder woman down the beach. Out in the moonlight, the statue was more wonderful than ever. There was something about that expression in stone that almost scared me. The curled stone lips, the sneer of the nose, the expression was more than a taunt, it seemed to jeer and invite at the same time — you've had women look over their shoulder at you like that? — and meanwhile the beauty of form rushed the blood to my forehead.

Rallston's voice came savage through his set teeth.

"Push, you idiot! Get her to the boat!"

If ever there was a madder kidnaping in history, I'd like to know it. It was easier sledding on the crusted sand. The beach sloped toward the water, and we skidded the drag at half a mile an hour, raising columns of white dust that stood up against the moon. The white dust was thick as gunpowder, acrid, bitter in the nostrils; twice I had to sneeze. I labored like a piano mover, darted nervous eyes at the sleeping town.

But a man will risk plenty when he's looking at a million dollars, and the statue was worth two million, or I was blind. When I thought of what the archeologists and art collectors would pay for the sculpture, desire gripped me like a drug. Rallston looked drugged, too. His gray-green eyes were shining as if coated with enamel. We were a pair, all right. A pair of deuces playing in a game with a joker.

Well, we got her down to the bum-boat, and we smuggled her aboard. We worked like pyramid builders to do it, I can promise you. Rotted tackle snapped like thread, had to be knotted in a dozen places. That decayed deck boom bent like a sapling bough as we hauled and tore our fingernails, elevating the cargo inboard and lowering her down the hatch.

Get a picture of us loading that statue on that wilderness shore. Rallston broke her ankle chains with the spear, and we hoisted her up and let her down. I groaned in fear of breaking the brittle statuary. Lowering her into the bum-boat's hold we splintered a chip from her shoulder, and it brought the tears to my eyes.

Down in the dusty gloom of the bargehold — a box of a place about big enough for fifty sacks of meal — we struggled like stevedores to stow her upright in a corner. I don't know where the moisture came from, for the thirst was swelling my tongue against my teeth, but the perspiration was guttering on both of us when we chinned ourselves out of the hatch, slapped down the hatch-cover and rushed to the thwart amidships to grab the oars. I guess I'd forgotten how tired I was. I guess I'd forgotten a lot of things. All I could think of was the living expression on that stone statue's face and what the art galleries would pay to see it.

"But we'll never make it," I groaned at Rallston as we pulled the barge out of the headland's shadow and set her blunt snout for open sea.

Off the bows that saffron fog was creeping in, and the long swells marched out from under the vapor banks like lava swishing molten out of steam. The barren headland, the junk-iron cliffs with that Valley of Death behind them, the Arab town at the end of the simitar beach made the backdrop for a play laid on the moon.

"If this *is* the Red Sea, we've miles out to the ship lane. Those Arabs will be after us like hounds when — "

Rallston laughed, and his laughter hardly sounded sane. Nothing was sane that midnight, I promise you.

"Suppose they do take after us — they didn't see us snaffle the woman, did they? There's other pirate ships on this waterway, and once in the fog we're safe."

My teeth were knocking together just the same, but premonitions aren't much good against thoughts of a million dollars. We pulled the blisters out on our palms, rowing out to reach that fog. We pulled with might and main, and the barge moseyed along like a Chinese junk, but we got there. I think the devil let us get there just to encourage us. Rallston had scuttled his re-

ligion for romance; I'd thrown over common sense for a fortune; both of us had fallen for the type of woman a man should
let be; the devil encouraged us to let us down because we needed
a lesson.

The lesson started just as we reached that yellow fog-bank.
A Lilliputian chorus of howls splitting the silence along the
shore. Torches dodging and darting along the beach. Arabs
came pouring down the miniature walls of that distant town like
fireflies swarming out of a hive. Guns snapped in crackling
strings like boxes of crackers suddenly exploding. They must
have seen us, because little fountains plunked and spurted in
our wake. Next minute their boats were out, oars flashing,
spreading across the water like a horde of many-legged water-
spiders heading seaward. A bullet cut an invisible violin-string
over my head.

"Row!" Rallston yelled. "They're after us!"

We stabbed our oars into the brine, and the fog plunged
over us at a swoop. The regatta was on!

It will be a long time before I forget that midnight row.
The mist of that excursion is still in my head, and the prints of
an oar-handle are branded on my palms. Have you ever been
rowing at night when the wind dies and leaves the sea running,
when everything is quiet above the surging water? Add fog to
the business and you have something downright uncanny. The
fog we burrowed into that night was mysterious as smoke from
Aladdin's lamp.

Shots crackled behind us as our bum-boat collided with the
fog-bank, and then it was precisely as if we had gone through a
wall. A wall of gauze spread in layers above the wave-tops; then
it was cotton, pulling, raveling, weaving around us as thick as
an old man's beard. Deeper in, the fog was banked in piles like
washed wool, great masses of aqueous wool heaped atop the
water by invisible hands.

The wool swirled over us, dripping, smothery, silent.
Kissed our faces, bandaged our heads, blurred Rallston to a

shadow at my side. We were buried. Wrapped in a goose-flesh, creaming smother, opaque as the glass of a frosted lamp-bulb. A queer incandescence shone through the stuff. It wasn't blind. Perhaps like light seen by a cataracted eye. And there were rainbows, vague as the colors in an opal, arching in the formless clouds, the sort of other-world rainbows that moonbeams would cast.

On the thwart beside me, Rallston was pulling his oar with the automatic fury of someone pumping a colossal handcar, and the teeth grinned in his errant face like a string of pearls.

"They'll never catch us now," he bawled at my ear. "Row! Don't slow down!"

We weren't slowing down because we'd never gone fast enough to admit any slowing, but an illusion of decreased momentum affected by fog was not dispelled by the armada I knew was whooping after us. I knew those Arab feluccas were coming like Indian war canoes, and I slammed my big blade in the sea with all the energy of fear. Don't think that barge with that shanghaied lady weighting the bows was any trifle to row. It wasn't any college shell. It plowed through the mist with all the elephantine grace of a New York garbage scow butting a head sea of mud.

Rallston feathered his oar and sat with his ears cocked, listening.

"Do you hear them coming?"

"I can't hear anything," I confessed.

It was remarkably quiet when we listened. We couldn't hear a trace of those bloodhounds we'd seen astern. We might have been barging through the sky, save for the wash of water hammocking by abeam, the little wallops of brine that smacked against the bow and scattered miniature showers across our necks.

"They've missed us all right," Rallston chuckled. "It's been at least two hours since we saw 'em last, and they're off our course or they'd have overhauled us long ago. All we've got to do now is pick up a ship for Suez."

You see how it was? We didn't know we were on the Red
Sea to begin with, but all we had to do was pick up a ship to Suez.

Of course there were a variety of other reasons why we might
never pick up that ship. Conceivably such a ship might pick us
up in the vapor and slice us like a buzz-saw cutting cheese. Or
we might be rowing in a circle. Or an Arab broadside might
catch us out of the mist. But we didn't think of that.

It doesn't do to navigate when you're in love, and we were
in love. Rallston was in love with the cynicism of our lady
passenger, and I was in love with her money. It would pay me
back for the rifles and equipment I'd lost. More than repay me.
Do you know what I was thinking as I rowed myself black and
blue in that fog? Not that I was a thief, I can tell you. I told myself
I was stealing the woman because she was a great work of art, a
super-masterpiece that belonged to the salons of the world.

And I was counting the dollars the salons would pay for
such a prize. The workmanship of the statue inspired me, but
the dollars intoxicated me. Paris. Nice. Monte Carlo. No more
grubbing with lizards. I had no more religion than my young
assistant collector, that night! I was drunk as I rowed that barge.

And at every mile and every hour, deeper and deeper in
the fog, I grew drunker. Not from anything to drink, either.
My mouth had been bone-dry when we'd launched the cruise,
and a few hours exercising at the sweeps had turned my tongue
to a herring.

The fog was something. Tantalizing. I wrung drops from
my cuffs, licked the beads from my wrists, but the taste of water
only aggravated thirst a hundred-fold. Just the devil's way of
keeping us going. I'd have bartered my soul for a glass of wine,
but every time I thought of the statue in the forward hold I forgot
I had a soul.

I guess the good Lord thought I'd better be reminded of it,
for I got a little jolt about then. Rallston shipped his oar, flung a
fist to my elbow, dragged me down on the seat, froze.

"Quiet!"

We hunkered down on the thwart and bulged our cheeks

with stifled breath. A sound of rhytmic splashing obtruded on watered hush. Cambridge, Oxford, two dozen racing crews were going by somewhere. We caught the murmurous cantata of many voices, and there was the merest suggestion of a shadow off to starboard, as of the passage of a phantom ship tacking through imagination.

"It's them," Rallston gritted after an interval of baited silence. "Damn them, they're headed straight out. We've got to turn north."

"I don't see any compass in our binnacle," I choked. "How do you mean, turn north?"

We weren't doing any loud talking, believe you me. Rallston's words barely touched my ear. "A head sea coming in from the west when we put out. Take it on the port beam, we're going north. Row like hell."

For an hour that seemed a century we rowed like hell with the barge growing heavier every drag. As an extra goad to effort, the fog began to tear away in spots, rip and fray into fog-dogs — holes in the vapor where moonlight shafted down from a glimpse of open sky and our oar-blades crunched through a patch of glittering sea dark as a whirlpool sighted at the bottom of a mine.

When we scowed through one of those openings we flattened like turtles on the thwart, holding breath, sick, expecting a fusillade from some mist-ambushed Arab craft to blow us out of water. But the enemy armada might have phantomed off into cloudland, set sail for the Pleiades. From the massed wool hemming us in there was only the sound of water underneath.

I don't know how long we played hide-and-seek through those fog-dogs, then, but I'd worn the flesh from my fingers, worked my spine numb and my tongue out — I'd have sworn we'd crossed the Atlantic — and I was dreaming of Paris again, when Rallston gave another cat-jump and blurted, "Land!"

I was a galley slave hanging on the oar-handle, cursing in disbelief. "Where?"

"Can't you hear what I hear, Farraday? Listen!"

"All I hear is running water," I husked. "I can't hear any
— "

Then I caught it. A far-off muttering that had forced its echo
through the fog from a distance of at least two miles, not unlike
the long roll of muffled marching drums beating across a valley
filled with rain.

Dilated, exultant, Rallston's eyes burned hot in his mist-
smudged face.

"Surf!" he cheered the whisper. "Surf on a beach!" Leaping
upright, he sent a triumphant glare across our bow, pointing a
shaky finger dead ahead. "That's Egypt, by God; we've made
the other side. We've done it, Farraday! Brought her over. Land!
We're saved!"

Only we weren't saved yet. Not by a jugful. Rather, not by
a boatful! His cheer wasn't out of his teeth when the barge broke
through a rift in the mist, drifted out into a patch of moonlight.
I don't know why I looked down at that moment. Not till then
did I realize my feet were wet; I suppose my subconscious mind
had been trying to tell me, but I'd been having too good a time
in Paris, been too busy exploring the fog for enemies, to pay attention to wet feet.

Well, I'd heard a sound of water under the fog, and it was
running, all right. Running right into the boat! Boiling up
through the bottom-boards and gurgling in through the seams
at about two quarts a minute. Too long that craft had been
beached in the tropic sun. The weather on that scrap-iron coast
had eaten the pitch and gnawed the timbering to punk. Those
planks were drinking in brine like thirsty blotting paper. The
bilge was up to my bootlaces when I looked, and I pulled my
feet out with a yell. Rallston looked down and squalled.

"Holy Moses! We're leaking!"

That barge was something more than leaking. Having
sprung one leak, the whole motheaten hull had opened the rest
of its seams; gone porous as the Dutch boy's dike. Stealthily,
lazily as a hippopotamus submerging, the craft had begun to
sink!

Well, we were in for it this time, and Paris in the spring vanished right out of the bubble in my head. Picture that situation if you can. A girl-crazy lunatic and a naturalist who should have known better trying to kidnap a stone goddess in a scow of cardboard. Fog on a lost planet sea, and fang-toothed Arab pirates liable to be anywhere, and the ship going down. Lord, how that bumboat was drinking in the brine. It liked the taste. It had started slowly and developed a liking, and now it was gulping the stuff by the gallon.

Rallston stared at his flooded shoetops and went white.

"Bail!" he yelled, giving me a shove that knocked me off the thwart. "I'll do the rowing. Get that water out of here. Bail like the devil."

He snatched the oars and started pulling like a madman, while I bailed in the sternsheets like Noah's pump. I used my sun helmet to scoop with, and I might as well have tried to empty the Indian Ocean with a soup spoon. All he water I could jettison simply ducked down under our keel and sneaked in again, bringing a fresh supply with it. The seams were widening by the second, and I labored like an up-and-down in a Scotch freighter, dipping and throwing, dipping and throwing, with no more result than to see the intake rise to my ankles and start for my shins.

"She's going down," I had to pant. "It's coming in faster all the time. She's up two inches since I started."

Rallston slammed the oars into the swells and pulled as if to uproot the sea from its bed.

"We've got to make that shore off there, d'you hear? We can't lose that woman now!"

"But we're sinking deeper," I had to groan a moment later. "It's up to my shins. The water must be in that hold forward, too. She's started a list in the head."

Rallston dropped the oars to snatch the helmet from my fingers. "You row! We can't sit out here and sink in this tub! If this fog wasn't on us we'd be in sight of land. Keep going, man! Keep going!"

I rowed and Rallston bailed. Rallston rowed and I bailed. We spelled off and panted and swore and rowed and bailed, and now that it had started the caper that bumboat kept filling like a bathtub under opened faucets, staggering up over the hills of brine and wallowing down the valleys, a little slower, a little logier at each successive swell.

For the following half hour we fought to beat that sea inside and out, but it had us coming and going. Inside the brine climbed inch by inch to our kneecaps. Outside the hurrying swells rushed out from under the fog, grew off the bow, swept by with the whoosh of liquid glass, and I groaned each time our blunt-nosed barge survived the assault.

Land was ahead of us somewhere, no doubt of that. An echo of combers on a beach as difficult of attainment as Paradise. It wasn't for those who took the easy road. Our barge was too heavy for that ocean in the clouds. At each new swell the drunken hulk would shudder and stagger and swallow another gallon.

"Get out of the trough," Rallston shouted at me from the stern. "Another like that last on the beam and we'll go down."

I pulled my arms out to get her around, but she seemed to be settling in glue by that time. reluctant to swing. Her head was leaden. It rose and sank on the heaving floor under the fog with no more buoyancy than concrete, lowering a little farther at each swell like the head of some sea monster getting sleepy.

Rowing that hulk took the buoyancy out of me, too. We wallowed down a sliding liquid valley smothered with fog, and it was all I could do to drag her up the other side. Rallston was throwing hatfulls of water forty feet over his shoulder, but his efforts could do nothing for those spread bottom boards. Over his knee-caps in water, he bent at the waist and started fumbling around under the bilge.

I yelled at him not to stop bailing, and he showed me a pair of eyes red as rubies in the sockets of a skull.

"I'm going to get that woman ashore if we drown in forty fathoms. It's too late to bail. We've got to lighten the boat."

You know how balloonists throw ballast out of the baskets

in the sky? You should have seen Rallston throwing ballast out of that sinking barge to keep us afloat in the clouds. First he got that iron spear we'd stolen from the Arab guard — dragged that spear out from under the thwart, splashed by me to scramble to the higher ground of the foredeck where he chopped down our mast at one whack. Crack! Sail, cordage, boom and tackle went overside, splashing off in the mist. The anchor went next, followed by the watercask, a length of chain, a box of rusted spikes, anything he could lay fingers on.

"Throw everything that's loose," Rallston screamed. "We're almost awash!"

The spear sailed from his fist and disappeared in the steam. Floundering aft, he dredged the bottom-boards for excess baggage, flinging overside a coil of waterlogged hawser, a carpenter's maul from God knew where, a link of chain, such rubbish as an urchin might discard from a pocket.

Do you think five pounds of junk more or less made any difference in that situation? I thought of the half-ton cargo in our forward hold, and it made me sick. Rallston stiffened upright in the sternsheets just then, and he must have been thinking of the same thing.

"There's not much else to throw out," he said in a high-pitched voice. "We're still sinking."

I didn't say anything. The water was lapping the thwart, and my mouth was filled with a taste like dry quinine.

"There's not much else to throw out," Rallston repeated in the same squeaky tone. "But her — " he pointed at the foredeck " — *and she's not going.*"

My lips cracked like an old cup as I grinned at him, nodding agreement. "Right. She's not going."

"Do you think I'd chuck that woman overboard after risking my life to get her?"

I shook my head. I could feel a little tendon throbbing under my left shoulder blade, and all the little hairs went tight and electric on my back. I whispered:

"I wouldn't chuck her overboard, myself."

"But there's too much weight," Rallston whispered. "Somebody's got to go."

I nodded, rising slowly from the thwart.

"And *she's* not the one of us that's going!" he squalled.

Water showered under our boots and we hit each other at the same time.

Now I'm not going to beg off responsibility in that assault by claiming I was crazy. I think we were both as crazy as bobcats when we went for each other — I'm certain we were — but it was the brand of craziness that comes from playing with money and wise women, and the judges won't take it as an excuse. What do you think the Admiralty Board would say of two boys who tried to throw each other overside to save a statue on a sinking barge?

Vividly I remember the pain of my knuckles landing on Rallston's jaw, the simultaneous explosion of stars as his own fist struck me between the eyes. *Wham!* That Australian's fist was chain-mailed. The blow drove me backward with the force of a donkey's kick, and flung me head-over-heels over the thwart, smack down under three feet of bilge.

The bath cleared my wits a little, and I came up draggled and coughing in time to catch Rallston's rebound from the stern. His face looked madder than the grimace of Cain. A thread of blood leaked from one splayed nostril where my knuckles had contacted, and his grin seemed composed of a thousand teeth.

Gabled under a roof of wet hair that streamed in two dark triangles on either temple, his eyes had contracted, dwindled to sharp points of green glass imbedded in a face hot as a boilerplate. Jaw out, snorting, fingers spread, he flung himself at me.

"She's mine! I found her, you perishin' jackal! Think you can pitch me overside, do you? She belongs to me!"

"You woman-crazy, triple-blasted fool!"

I howled, trying to fist him off. We fought. Slashed and slugged, wrestled, kicked, tore, each striving to knock the other over the gunwales. We weren't the first young men to go mad over a million dollars and a woman. In a way, our supercargo

in the hold was both. Grimly, murderously, deadly as rival animals, we fought. Wrist-twists and rabbit-punches. Snarling and
circling for position. Leaping in for the catch. Howling backwards with kicked shins. Rallston's fingers closed like locked
manacles on my throat, and I drove my knee into his midriff, a
blow that spun him around like a dervish.

Locked together, we fell, ploughed along the bottom-
boards, rolling about under water, arms twined, legs hooked,
strangling, thrashing, eyes bugged, and cheeks distended for
want of air. We broke, kicked apart, plunged to our feet and
danced back, shoulders bunched, heads down, measuring the
second for another charge.

"Get off! Get off!" Rallston screamed at me. "You're sinking
the barge, sinking my woman — "

"I'll go down with the boat if she goes," I promised him
furiously. "But you're going overboard first — "

As he lunged at me then, I wrenched an oar from the rowing
lock, jumped back, struck him across the mouth. He caught the
blade in his hands, deflecting the blow, jerking me off balance.
Dodging down, he snatched the second oar before I could stop
him; planted the rounded handle in his arm-pit, charged me
with blade pointed like a lance.

Whip! Crack! Slash! I'd like to have been a disinterested wit-
ness to the duel that followed. I'd like to have seen that battle
aboard a barge sinking under opalescent fog, the oar-blades
stabbing, whipping parabolas of light through mist, slashing
together overhead, splinters shearing, slivers flying, the crack
of wood on wood, the smack of wood on bone. What a joust that
was! What a gallant contest of knights! What a lady for a prize,
and what a field of honor! It sickens me to think of it now.

It sickens me to remember that the only thing in my mind
throughout that battle was the million-dollar masterpiece in the
hold at my back. When I thought of that precious image going
to Davy Jones, I yelled and tried to break my oar over Rallston's
head. Blow for blow, he gave me as good as he got, sometimes
better. A score of times we teetered on the gunwale, whaling,

fighting to keep balance, to stay aboard. There weren't any Marquis of Queensbury rules in that brawl. Eye for eye, tooth for tooth, it was. At that you couldn't understand unless you'd seen the workmanship, the genius in the absolute perfection of that statue. Unless you'd seen the living expression in that sculptured woman's face.

All this time the barge was wallowing lower and lower in that swinging brine, lurching down a jolt at each wave. Every time we felt another lurch we went at it with doubled fury. If we'd been fresh at the start we'd have murdered each other first whack, but we'd been up too late the night before, worked too hard on empty stomachs and shriveled throats. I've an idea our blows and jabs were more sluggish than they seemed. Perhaps mental exhaustion sustained an illusion of top speed action that wasn't real, but the pain was authentic enough.

Our faces were cut open, and our fists red. Shirts sheared to tatters on our backs. I split my oar-blade on the side of Rallston's jaw, while he answered the blow with a slam on my head that nearly drove me through the leaky timbers of the bottom. Parrying, flailing. I forced him reeling into the stern. Back at me he charged, cutting strokes through mist that would have sliced my head like a melon if they'd landed.

"Damn you, Farraday! She's mine — "

"Over you go! Try that — that — another — "

Older men wouldn't have lasted. Only healthy young animals could give and take such a pounding. In those days I was wiry, and my skull topped Rallston's by an inch. Life in the open had stored a lot of energy in my hide. He was built for an athlete, muscled like an orang-utan. My blows only enraged and confused him. His vitality seemed unquenchable. I punished his arms with criss-cross strokes, pounded his knuckles, couldn't chop his weapon from his fists. He beat me to my knees, crushed the ears flat on my head, brought the eyebrows swelled down over my lids, but he couldn't whip me out of that barge.

In the mist the oar-blades were flashing crimson. Water

churning around our knees clouded maroon. Chips flew. Lungs whined. Believe me, I can't tell you how long the fight lasted, any more than I can tell you how long we'd been out in that floundering bumboat. Time loses outline in fog, and our battle stopped the clock. We might have fought five minutes, ten, but it seemed to carry on for hours, a year. A drear, nightmarish quality came into that fog-screened conflict. The nightmare of Rallston's unstoppable attacks. The nightmare of standing again and once more to beat him back.

The feeling was pounded out of me. My hands were without nerves. I know that battle lasted until even the illusion of speed was dissipated and the power to stand up and swing my oar seemed to come from some mysterious element outside my whipped frame, some evil sustenance loaned me by a far, black star. It takes a lot of punishment to rid the human body of avarice, and the last fight between men on this world will take place because of greed.

The barge was on her last legs, too. Brine was slopping over the gunwales, and the seas slanted tall, gathering power for their own killing punch. A big swell came rushing out of the fog, but the drowning hulk was every bit as stubborn as the fools fighting across her thwart. The punch-drunk hull gave a stagger and a groan, shook streams of brine from her drooping head, wallowed over the crest and lifted her foaming pug-nose clear for another gasp.

Crying that I'd sunk her, Rallston rushed me with swinging oar; caught me a screeching wallop across the cheekbone. Wood broke to kindling on my face, and thrown sidewise, shocked wide awake with pain, I brought my own oar down on his scalp with a smash that shivered my oar-blade to broom-straws. Both of us plunged over backwards; caught at the gunwale; hung. I can see it as if it happened yesterday — that untamed Australian pulling himself up to the rowing seat, panting and gargling, hauling himself together piece by piece as if broken bones were joining themselves under his skin, the effort

standing green veins on his forehead, bringing the tongue
through his teeth, dragging himself upright with his oar for a
crutch, inevitably, monstrously on his feet.

You know the picture of the dying Gaul? It made me think
of that, Rallston coming up on his broken weapon. Head bloody,
yes, and bowed. But on his feet. The tears scalded my eyes at
seeing him there, and I cursed him as you'd curse an apparition,
hauling my own carcass out of the bilge, forcing my own gruelled
legs to a stand.

Propped on our oars, water gushing around our knees,
backs sagged, faces dripping scarlet, we stood with the thwart
separating us, eye to eye in the fog, two ruined gladiators sinking
in our own misguided boots.

"Mine!" He brought the words with red bubbles through
his teeth. "The woman — all — mine — "

"No, Rallston. No — " My head was too sick to shake. "No!"

As if by a common reflex we lifted the oars. Stood swaying.
Lurched. Dropped our weapons. Fell together like scarecrows
deprived of their wooden spines. Splash! Dropped like two cut-
down bags of meal across the rowing seat.

A dark hill of water swept out of the mists to starboard, and
the finish came.

But it didn't come from the sea. That finish came out of the
fog. A chorus of howls breaking loose in the smother off the
bow. The *plash, plash, plash* of a multitude of paddles. Shadows
shooting in from all directions like mammoth shark-fins skating
up through mist. Rows and files of merciless brown faces conjured out of vapor, and then the whole yowling regatta of dhows,
nuggers, feluccas and sampans circling around us and engulf-
ing us in a traffic jam as wild as a tie-up on the Yangtze Kiang.

I never saw so many rifles aimed at my head at one time. So
many brandished knives. A hook-beaked Arab colossus, brown
as a penny, black-whiskered, wearing a turban, was a figurehead posed in the foresheets of the nearest boat. His simitar
looked bigger than the moon. He had grabbed up to heaven

and caught that tremendous crescent in his hand. He let out a roar of coughing Arabic at his boatmen; his galley scraped alongside our half-submerged stern and he boarded us with the agility of a corsair, leaping at Rallston and me, simitar upraised.

"The image," he roared in guttural English. "We come for the sacred image, *feringi!* Return thy theft quickly, spawn of unholiness, and prepare to die!"

Myself, I prepared to die. I found no time to wonder at this Arabian behemoth's English, unexpected to that climax as a British accent on Mars. I didn't even wonder why our barge didn't plunge straight down under the weight of the pirate and his simitar. My neck was bared under that moon-sized blade, and I was too lame and tired to move. If the flooded bumboat didn't sink, my heart did then, and I couldn't lift my head off the thwart.

Rallston moved. I tell you, that Australian devil had more damnation left in his hide than a wounded tiger. He lifted his broken head, and even laughed. Sprawled beside me on the rowing seat, he reared up at the headsman towering over us and chewed a sound of mirth through his teeth.

"I don't know what you're talking about," he chattered at Blackbeard, "but if you don't get off this boat in half a nip she'll sink to the bottom. You understand English, you whisker-faced shark? Then understand you're talking to Captain Rallston of his Britannic Majesty's Corps of Signals and this is Lieutenant Farraday of the American Observation Service. There's an official camera under this seat to prove it, understand? We're on military assignment and got wrecked in this fog, and by God, if you know what's good for you, you'll call off your pirates and have us put ashore."

It was a good bluff. A remarkable bluff. That boy was a super salesman, and when I think of how he blustered and stalled, half fainting and trapped on that foundering barge, I have to take my hat off to his gall. We were caught with the goods, but that superannuated lady-stealer wasn't licked yet. If he could stall a few more seconds the evidence would go down like the *Titanic* and we might get away.

He conjured a look of innocence on his pounded face that would have done credit to a saint. You'd have thought this Arab chieftain was no more than some irate papa who'd caught Rallston eloping with his daughter, but the girl was safely hidden behind the scenes. Image? What image did our visiting admiral mean? Sacred image? Where?

It didn't fool Blackbeard any more than Rallston had expected it would — that sheik knew we weren't any Captain Rallston and Lieutenant Farraday innocently wrecked to black eyes and crushed noses in the fog. What Rallston did expect was that our bumboat would go down like a plummet, and the bumboat refused to oblige. It wallowed level with the waterline while brine burbled over the stern and we clung to the thwart like rats on a raft. Blackbeard belted his simitar on a sash under his cloak and listened to Rallston's story with folded arms. Then,

"Move once," he snarled, "and my men will shoot the truthless heads from your shoulders. *Wah!* That would be a mercy compared to the tortures awaiting those thieves who dared steal the ancient image from the tribe of Haram esh-Shereef! The proof of that guilt will not be far distant, *feringi*, and by Allah's Holy Prophet! I think your blood will flow when I see what cargo lies hidden beneath that forward hatch!"

He bellowed at his followers to train their rifles for a broadside, then went scrambling and splashing to the bumboat's foredeck, and ripped up the hatchcover at a yank. He jumped down the hatch with a savage yell, and his armada of pirates shrieked with the glad prospect of a chance to torture the Christians when they saw him go. It was all up now. Overhead the fog was dissolving in watery light as if the dawn were trying to get through and make two scoundrels sorry they were seeing it for the last time. I pushed my bruised face down on the thwart, cold to the marrow with suspense.

"Rallston," I gibed him bitterly, "what do you think of your dream-girl, your daring wonder-woman, now? I wish I'd killed you before they do; it was your wonderful romantic ideas that got us into this."

"I won't go down prayin', anyway," he sneered from a corner of his bruised mouth. "I'll leave you do the howlin' to heaven for a miracle that won't come. I'll go to the devil like a man."

There was a submarine splash as Blackbeard lit in the flooded hold, and I could hear Rallston cursing the hulk because it didn't sink. I listened to that Arab chief trampling and wading down under the hatch; heard snorts, muffled exclamations, a fierce yell. Then I don't exactly recall how it happened. To Judgment Day I'll never forget the sight of that Arab's head bellowing up out of that hatch, the picture of him climbing up to the foredeck like a buffalo rising from a manhole, turban over one ear, cloak soaked to the armpits from immersion down below, paddling, puffing, his face — have you ever seen an Arab who found himself cheated in a deal? An Arab who wagered the wrong way?

He struck his forehead with a fist and glared dramatically up at the sky. Despair, humiliation, anxiety, fury fought for predominance on his features. It takes a raging Arab to speak in a voice of humility. He wrung his hands, stamped at Rallston and me, and wrung his hands. Truly, there had been a wretched mistake. Allah forgive this unwarranted assault on the *feringi*. It was the fog, the cursed fog which deluded the eye, making lambs appear as wolves.

Could Captain Rallston and Lieutenant the *Amerikani* and the emperors of both England and America — on whom be the blessing — pardon him an error caused by fog? Of course, now the daylight was coming, we did not in the least resemble thieves. But had we by chance passed other small boats in the dark? What? The *feringi* had seen many others? Then by the Three-Fingered Hand of the Wife of the Prophet, there was no more time to lose! He would be delighted to assist us to shore, but there was not the time.

Salaam! Salaam! Farewell!

My next visual impression, that Blackbeard figurehead was back in the bows of its felucca. I give you my word, that Arab made a flying leap back to his own boat; I saw the pointed rifles withdraw like claws going into sheaths; saw those wolf-faced boatmen snatch their oars, sails go up like flags, paddles smack into the sea. Bag and baggage, that Arab pirate took leave.

He took the fog with him. His boats towed it after them as they rocked away, pulling the vapors astern to screen their departure. I was aware of pale blue sky opening overhead, a high bird planing in aery daylight. Sunlight sifted fans of gold over a cloud to warm a spreading view of waves. In the east where the fog was retreating, the Arabs were no longer visible. For a long time I lay immobile, staring at the place where Blackbeard and his fleet had gone.

Then I turned my head very carefully, and surprised a coastline off the bow. Not half a mile away a glimmering beach, where quiet surf laundered white rocks and olive trees stood green atop a cliff and distant hills sloped violet and purple in bright upper air.

The shore looked virtuous and peaceful. It had no affinity to that coast of our embarkation. Sunshine on water. Sparkling wavelets. Goats posed on rocks, and there was a pastel house among the olives. We had drifted from a land of goblins into another sphere. Only the sunken hulk bearing us toward this sunny beach remained as evidence to last night's nightmare.

"Rallston," I whispered tentatively, wanting to make sure.

But it wasn't a dream. He voiced a sound like a croak to let me know he was there, and I screwed around on the seat to find him kneeling on the bottom-boards in bilge, arms hugging the thwart as if afraid to let go, head thrust forward, eyes staring. Drying brine had left a chemical deposit like diamond-dust splarkling in the tangles of his hair, so that his head glowed in the sun as if immortally crowned by some manner of halo. His face looked something immortal, too, crusted, swollen, harlequinned with rainbow-colored welts. His eyes, stuck in their sockets, were made of glass.

"Farraday," he whispered, "did you see some Arabs around here?"

"I thought — "

"Did a big black-whiskered devil jump down into the hold and — and climb out and go away?"

"It seemed to me — "

"Come on."

The hatch was open, and we crawled on hands and knees. Rallston groaned as he chinned himself down, and as I lowered myself after him, day came across the sky in a yellow blaze and the air was filled with light. You can't dream tropical sunlight, but the scene in that bumboat's flooded cargo hold had to be a dream. Sunshine poured down through the hatch overhead to fill the square enclosure with brilliance, and the water was clear and crystalline as a sea cave under the Bermudas. That six-by-six hold was shoulder-deep in water, water that had leaked in through the seams in the hull, but the planking was solid on the walls and bottom, and a half-ton statue too heavy for a single man to lift can't get out through cracks.

Now laugh when I tell you that statue wasn't there. Laugh when I tell you that wonderful sculptured woman with her "come get me, I dare you" expression wasn't standing in the corner where Rallston and I had stowed her. No man could have budged that image. It had wanted block and tackle to get her aboard. Rallston hadn't touched her, nor had I; and Blackbeard had departed with empty hands. The statue had departed, too. She wasn't in her corner, or the other three corners; she wasn't on the floor. But there was something about the size of a lily pad and about the thickness of thin pie crust floating over the surface where the woman had been.

I stood with Rallston chest-deep in the water of that hold, sunlight cracking down through the hatch and ricochetting in white crescents off the little wavelets to make dancing reflections on the deck-timbers overhead — I stood with Rallston in that boxed-in pond, and we stared. How we stared!

It wasn't any pie crust, I can tell you. Can you imagine the skim of some white powder floating on the surface of a pool? Or the skin of a human face, the top-layer, say, of a death mask set floating in brine? The back of that mask was gone. The body wasn't there. Just the last outer film, the merest suggestion of that face remained afloat, as if sketched on the eddying ripples by a few strokes of dusty chalk.

"Look!" Rallston screamed. "Look!"

I saw it, all right. Misty as a photograph in smoke. An expression set adrift. The face of a woman looking over her shoulder, daring someone to "get" her — a mirage looking up at us from crystalline brine. Rallston's cry tore out of his throat in one exorcised devil of sound. Together we sprang. Together we rushed at that thing, hands out, like children trying to catch a reflection in a lake.

I caught it, too. How I caught it! I tripped over Rallston's boots and dived headlong, full face into that smoky expression, smack on the mouth. Those phantom lips in a phantom sneer! Can you see how it was? My face went into that thing and I closed howling lips on a mouthful of brine I'll not forget when the last trump blows. I swallowed a gulp of seawater that would have sickened a whale. I broke that pie crust face into a million particles; drank half of it; spluttered to the surface with that "come get me, I dare you" expression showering out of my fingers, pouring through my hair.

Rallston got some of it himself. He flung a hand to his mouth and went up out of the hatch as if fired from a catapult. He was scrubbing his face when I pulled out of the bath to stand beside him, and that Australian renegade looked sick as a dog. Both of us did.

"Melted," he whispered. "My God — "

"That's why the barge didn't sink," I groaned. "This *isn't* the Red Sea! Do you know that coast over there?"

"I know," he said thickly. "Palestine! It's the *Dead* Sea!"

"That valley last night — "

"Gomorrah!"

He was praying on his knees when I went overboard. He fell to his knees as if he'd been sniped through the spine, and as I swam for the beach I looked back and saw him there. Kneeling on the deck of that half-sunk barge, face to the sky.

I didn't look back again. On the beach, I ran. There would be a well near that house among the olives, and I wanted a drink to wash that woman's expression from my mouth. But I'll never wash it out. Never! To this day my mouth burns with the taste, and I can see her face, defiant still, as my face fell to smash it in that bumboat's bilge. . . .

When Farraday stopped speaking, the twilight had melted to darkness in a miracle of its own, the Red Sea vanished to a path of bubbling phosphorus in the liner's wake. The tall mountain abeam was a shadow under a star, and somewhere within reach of that shadow, before the days of the Suez Canal, the Children of Israel had run dry-shod between waves, while the following chariots of Pharoah were engulfed.

A bar of yellow light came from the steering-engine house and put a shining hard scar down the naturalist's profiled jaw. Mendel, the metallurgist, stared at his companion's face. His lips felt cold on the question.

"You mean that statue — it dissolved?"

Farraday nodded. "The water finished what those fanatical Arabs had been preserving in that cave for centuries. That southern coast of the Dead Sea goes back in history. It isn't a part of Palestine you read about in guide books. Nobody'd go there but a couple of young fools who'd lost their way. That land was cursed in Genesis."

The metallurgist winced as Farraday gripped him by the shoulder.

"You and your winds and tides!" the naturalist rasped. "You'll say some wandering Greek in the days of Praxiteles carved that image out of rock and left it there. Well, Praxiteles was an amateur compared to the hand that did that sculpturing. The greatest sculptor in the universe did that statue. Only the greatest creative artist in the universe could have captured that 'come get me, I dare you' expression in rock.''

Farraday's eyes were bleak in the dimness. "And what kind of rock melts away? What kind of rock would disappear in the hold of a sinking bumboat and run out through the cracks? Not the kind of rock that Rallston's faith is built on, I can promise you. That atheistic, romance-crazy Australian was on his knees when I left him that day, and he's praying yet, from one end of Australia to the other. They say he's the greatest evangelist to ever start a crowd down the sawdust trail — his wife is a shy little woman who plays the organ — and a man has to be pretty sincere to pray in public these hardbitten days. I heard him recently on the radio, and what do you think his sermons are about? Miracles! His belief in miracles! Do you know what he uses for his text?"

Cold prickles moved up the metallurgist's skin. He waited with his mouth open a little.

Farraday was pointing toward the coast that was a shadow under a star, pointing in the direction of Arabia and the country beyond Arabia and the sea beyond that. His voice was low, husky on the quoted passage.

" '*And it came to pass . . . that he said, Escape for thy life, look not behind thee, neither stay thou in all the plain; escape to the mountain lest thou be consumed. . . . But Lot's wife looked back from behind him, and she became a pillar of salt.*' "

THE VOODOO EXPRESS

A Haitian Novelette
by
Theodore Roscoe

THE VOODOO EXPRESS

PROLOGUE

"Blood," said the cotton buyer, "will tell."

That was the remark that invited McCord's amazing story. That and the liquid-blue dusk and the dim, haunting echo of native drums beating somewhere up on the mountain behind the town where the lavender twilight deepened. A melon-colored moon was making Port-au-Prince and the bay below us more unreal than ever.

Our mulatto *garçon* came up the veranda with a tray of green swizzles, his feet making far less noise than his crinkling starched jacket. As he handed us our drinks he paused, listened, heard the drums; and I saw him smile. His retreat was a lazy-footed and soundless escape through shadows.

"There you have it!" the cotton buyer pointed his cigar. "Take that fellow there. Looks like a Frenchman, don't he? And civilized. But you saw how he went through them doors when he heard them drums? Just give him a smell of those drums and he goes right back to the bush; walkin' like a cat in the dark. Same as all these Haitians. A native is always a native when it comes to the test."

"I don't know, it may be the country gets in a fellow," the lank oil man from Texas suggested. "I think folks are sort of victims of where they live. Shape up to their environment. Now down here in the West Indies — heat, fever — you know how the tropics are — "

"It just brings out what's already in a fellow's blood," the florid cotton buyer insisted. "You take these creoles down here in the Islands — Guadeloupe, Jamaica, Trinidad. Give 'em a

71

chance, like in Haiti, here, and they go right back to type. Beat
voodoo drums and worship ghosts just like their ancestors did
in the Congo. Go back to type. Heredity. It always comes out
sooner or later. The tropics are the test, see?"

"Reminds me of a fellow I used to know down here," John
McCord said. "I was over in Cap Haitien surveying at the time.
Going to construct a coast road. Had a contract and my own
civil engineering firm. But the road job had encountered snags
and I ran a trading post on the side — sisal, coffee, sugar cane,
mahogany, what have you.

"Those were lively days for Americans in Haiti. Fifteen
years before that there'd been a typical banana republic revolution. Haiti is a lot more civilized today, but back in the World
War I era it was pretty primitive. A mob had murdered the black
President in Port-au-Prince. The United States had intervened,
and the Haitians didn't like Americans a little bit. Meantime
my trading affairs were getting tangled. I needed a partner
badly. But there weren't many Americans around anxious to
reside in Haiti those days. It was then this chap I'm speaking of
drifted in, and joined up with me. There's a story about that
guy, believe me."

McCord leaned forward, brushing back his thick, copper
hair, his blue eyes bright with memory. "You think you've heard
of some incredible adventures? Well, this one has a lot to do
with what we've been talking about, but in a way you won't
suspect. A lot to do with some other unsuspected things, too.
Pirate gold mixed with occult ritual, for instance. Ever hear the
legend of the Voodoo Express? I'll bet it's the weirdest story you
ever heard. Listen — "

The cotton buyer, the oil man and the rest of us there in the
Port-au-Prince Explorer's Club, we listened! McCord hadn't
exaggerated. The tropic dark, with its scent of sea and jungle,
whispered around the veranda. Far up the mountain behind
Port-au-Prince the Haitian drums throbbed a telegraph message
across the night. McCord's voice came at us out of shadow;
weaving this weird tale. . . .

CHAPTER I

Yole was his name. Conrad Yole. The consul over at Cap Haitien knew I was hard up for a business partner and sent Yole over to see me.

"Just the chap you've been looking for, McCord," the consul told me. "Knows the islands like an open book. He's been around 'em all, doing government survey and what not for this country an' that. You couldn't get a better man. He's lived in the Caribbean long as I can remember, and he's a great hand with the island people."

Yole was just what I wanted; and as he was broke and out of a job at the time, he eagerly came in with me. We knocked together an office, and business picked up. Yole certainly knew the territory. Talked all the dialects from Aruba to Dominica and could yak in Virgin Island Danish, Martinique French or Haitian creole as easily as he spoke English. He seemed to understand the psychology, too; knew a lot about their ways of doing business and a lot about their folklore.

I guessed him as one of those wandering expatriates who never can stay very long in one place, always harps about "going back to the States to settle down," and never does. He was always restless, scanning the waterfront and watching ship-smoke on the horizon with that far-away look in his eye. A shrewd negotiator, good chap to live with, but after six months I began to realize something was eating him.

In the first place he never told me much about himself. Usually a partner in some out-of-the-way hole opens up over a glass or two and hauls out a thumb-smeared photograph of his girl or his mother or his kid brother and talks about "going

73

CAP HAÏTIEN

MORNE LUNE

HAITI

ARCHAÏE

PORT-AU-PRINCE

JACMEL

home." Not Yole. I knew he came from Philadelphia. Had grad-
uated from Swarthmore, and had an engineer's degree from
Rensselaer Poly. But that was all he ever divulged. Five times a
day he might grumble the old bromide about going to the States.
But he never seemed to care what part of America he settled in
so long as it wasn't Haiti. He never referred to family or con-
fided any background detail.

"Soon as we clean up here, McCord," he'd declare, "I'm
getting out. I don't like this primitive creole republic."

Haiti wasn't exactly anybody's idea of heaven, and in those
days, as I said, it was liable to be uncomfortable for Americans.
It gave me the creeps to think how the Haitians had jumped on
the president, Guillaume Sam, and chopped him to mince meat.
Nothing can be more dangerous than a mob out for blood when
it really gets rampaging. One old granny had lopped off Guillaume's head with a machete and carried the thing across Port-
au-Prince with her, and another lady was reported to have dug
the president's heart out with a knife. The U.S. Marines had
been rushed into Haiti to put down the revolution. It didn't help
for our Government to wangle the ambush assassination of
Haitian rebel leader Benoit Batraville. The gunfire of guerrilla
warfare still echoed in the jungles on the Haiti-Santo Domingo
border. Every creole citizen in Cap Haitien paraded around
with a butcher knife. Angry drums uttered threats in the mountains. And I never left the house without my Colt. 45.

Yole, however, never carried a gun. He wasn't afraid of
the Haitians. They'd come down from the hills on market days
loaded with more knives than a scissors-grinder. They'd crowd
the street before our office and hand us some mighty mean stares.
Yole dealt with them and bullied them around without batting
an eye. Nights he'd go strolling the crowded waterfront unarmed
and bumping them out of his way. He made no bones about it
with them. He told them they were his inferiors with every
gesture he made. That was a dangerous thing to tell those Haitians. Creoles especially. They glared daggers at Conrad Yole,
but it didn't seem to scare him a trifle.

"I'm not afraid of these creole peasants," he declared. "I'm an American! I tell you, that's all you've got to show 'em, and they'll doff their caps to you smart as you please."

Then what disturbed him? Somewhere deep down inside of Yole there was an anxiety. Sometimes I'd catch the look of it in his demeanor. Our veranda overlooked a little bay with a headland, and nights you could see the lights of vessels in Windward Passage. More than once I discovered Yole standing in the dusk, twisting the veranda rail with white, knotted hands, his eyes hungry on some cruise ship steaming north to the States.

Another time I surprised him standing there in the gloom, and I got a real shock. Cap Haitien was blue with twilight — one of those tropic twilights after a rain when the air is perfumed with the smell of wet flowers and earth, and the sky is like a painting and you can almost hear green things growing in the jungle. There wasn't any wind to speak of, and in the crystal stillness the smoke from the hut chimneys in the town below rode straight up to the sky. Shafts of lavender light slanted down the horizon westward. The scrabble of the town was blurred with indigo. And the jungle behind our bungalow was purple and green, and the lofty mountain beyond was a dim, blue shadow with a nest of rose-tinted clouds on its peak. Away up there on the mountain somewhere a native drum was booming, faint as the throb of your pulse.

Only in Haiti are you fortunate enough to enjoy a scene like that, and it made me want to draw a cool, deep breath, feeling glad I was alive. Then I sighted Yole standing at the end of the veranda. A cool, deep breath? The man was breathing out gusts of hot steam. His hands were fastened to the railing. His face was etched in profile against the twilight, head jerked back on his neck, brown hair flung aside from his forehead, lips parted, panting like a landed bass. If ever I saw stark fright stamped on a man's countenance, I saw it then on Yole's.

The man was terrified. The shock in his face shot a shiver right down to my heels. It wasn't decent to stare at his fear like that, but I couldn't move to sneak away. The veranda almost quivered with his outlandish breathing, and there was no other sound save the distant pounding of that mountain drum. I was never to forget that scene and sound. I stood there a long time waiting for Yole to either faint of terror or move, and I was to hear that drumming again.

Boom! Boom! Boom! Three faint, lingering, dull-toned echoes. Then three short, skip-beat concussions. *Bum-bum-bum!* You get it? *Boom!—Boom!—Boom! Bum-bum-bum!* Like that. That faint sound of drums and Yole's asthmatic gasps. With that awful look of fear contorting his face.

It came over me in sudden revelation. What was scaring the man. That mountain drum wasn't beating out a signal for war. I'd heard that same drum-beat on many a previous evening, and there'd been no uprising afterward. The war drums had a different tone, too. This was some voodoo tom-tom going on up there on the ridge. A local dance. A few creole hillmen getting together to sacrifice a chicken and burn some harmless candles. Voodoo rites were common enough with the hill people. But nothing to make a man's teeth clack like dice in his jaw.

Yole's jaw had really begun to rattle, for a fact. He was standing in his shirt sleeves, and I remember how the sweat pasted the linen to his shoulders. I must have managed to move, for suddenly he heard me and spun around; and I saw sweatbands were like a jeweled diadem on his forehead. The eyes in his head were just glowing with fear, and he made a stride at me, catching my arm.

"McCord!" he blurted. "McCord, I've got to get out of here; out of Haiti! Listen, McCord, I'm through!"

His face, under ordinary circumstances rugged and tanned, was like dripping wax, greenish under the eyes.

"Good heavens, Yole, what's the matter?" I cried. "What the devil's wrong? You look like you'd seen a . . . "

He yelled. "I'm all right. Just fed up, that's all. Fed up! Sick of these damned natives and their damned drums and all the rest of it! I hate it, see? Why shouldn't I? I'm an American! A damned good one — without any business sticking around this rotten jungle country. I" — his voice dropped suddenly to a whisper, and his fingers loosened on my sleeve — "I'm just sick to death of the place, that's all. Reckon I've got a little fever, maybe. A civilized man can't stand this island, McCord. I've stuck around here too long. I'm fed up right to the neck!"

"Yole!" I took his wrist, and the skin was like melting ice. "You're scared, man. What the devil frightened you so?"

"Nothing!" He pushed me off. "I'm not scared. What's there to scare me about this rotten island. I tell you, I'm fed up. I'm getting out of here. No place for a civilized man, see? I'm sorry, McCord, but I'm leaving. Tomorrow. I'm clearing out."

Well, maybe that was all there was to it. A touch of fever and a desire to go north. I'd seen men act like that before. Men who'd lived in some foreign country for years, then suddenly got homesick and washed up without warning. Probably by tomorrow Yole would be over it. Swallow a pint of rum and forget all about leaving.

But he didn't get over it. He swallowed a jug of rum, but it didn't help. He reeled into the bungalow and put on a necktie and a sports coat he'd had sent down from New York. Yole had always been fussy about his dress; careful to have on hand the latest American fashions and flaunt them in the face of the Haitians in town. Now he stumbled around like a wild man, yelling at the house boy to shine up his boots, pawing in his duffle to find his derby hat and cane.

I could hear him shouting at the boy. "Come on, you ruffian! Where's that derby? Hurry, you lazy creole loafer. I told you to keep those shoes polished, you barefoot baboon! Say, 'sir' when you answer, or I'll knock that head off your shoulders! And bring me that other jug. Quick! You're not working for some sleep-in-the-sun cotton-picker!"

In the end he came out on the veranda with a breath you could notice a mile off, and dressed like a Broadway matinée idol of the Roaring Twenties. I'd glimpsed him through the veranda blinds, scrubbing at his face till it glistened; panting as

he manicured his nails; combing his black hair with military brushes till it gleamed like patent leather; then finishing off the rum. Now he wore a smart foulard tie, sports coat and flannels, his derby and his cane. You can imagine how inappropriate that costume looked on that bungalow veranda against a background of cane-bottom chairs, potted rubber plants and a kerosene lamp with a million insects blundering against the chimney.

"I'm going to the Officer's Club," he told me, a lot calmer than he'd been a half hour before. "The boy will pack my stuff and I'll make arrangements to catch the mail boat tomorrow night. I'll work with you tomorrow and help you straighten out the books. Don't look so blanked, old man. I hate to leave, because the business was doing all right, but you can find another partner. I'm sorry, but I'm all washed up."

The club he was going to was one of those pathetic institutions you find in foreign holes. One of those places where whites — "Only Aryans Allowed" — could congregate and thumb over monthy-old periodicals from home and play bridge and drink Planter's punch and talk about what's doing in the White House, and create a little air of superiority over their subordinate surroundings. Naturally enough excluded natives resent such an air of superiority; and the dark-skinned citizens of Haiti particularly resented it.

Yole had always played it up, was forever going into the club when he wasn't on the beach with his eyes on the horizon; and that night he played it to the hilt. I heard his shoes go squeaking down the path to town; and, still shaking from the shock he'd handed me earlier in the evening, I decided I'd better follow him.

I'd learned to like Yole, and I didn't want him jumped by a machete-wielding Haitian or two who might take the opportunity to resent his domineering. Buckling on my Colt for companionship, I trailed him.

Trailing him wasn't hard. Have you ever seen a drunken sailor in a foreign port? It takes one to toss out his chest, swing a

cane and go into a sea-roll with belligerent chips on both shoulders. Yole went into Cap Haitien that night with a swagger guar-
anteed to challenge trouble. An exaggerated, super macho cock-
of-the-walk march.

He lorded it through a crowd of Haitians down in the public
square; barged into the club like a John Wayne on a binge. And
there he got into an American complex for fair. I managed to
get planted in a corner where he didn't see me, and I watched
him. Whisky neat with a rum chaser. "Where's the New York
Times, old man?" to the Irishman back of the bar. "Have a look
at the Broadway shows. Times Square! There's the place for a
white man! Not a dump like this mud-hole!"

A good American. Fourth of July Yankee. He kept it up,
and the whisky and rum along with it. Hoped he'd always be a
good American. Three cheers for the red, white and blue.
Heaven only knew why white men hung around Haiti when
there was a place like Manhattan to live in, a place where folks
were civilized and wore shoes. New York, where people didn't
live in grass huts and beat drums, rattle gourds and worship
goats.

Midnight and he was still carrying on, his table crowded
with emptied bottles. His audience had long since been reduced
to two — me and the bored bartender. That didn't squelch his
Yankee Doodle Dandy act.

"Another bottle, Pat. Here's to the good old U.S.A. — there's
the place. Haiti's a Caribbean cesspool. By heaven, I'm leaving
tomorrow! Going to the States where there's decent hotels and
theaters and everyone wears shoes."

It was the "shoes" that finally penetrated. If there was one
thing that breached the gap between savagery and civilization,
in the mind of a Haitian native, it was a pair of shoes. The poor
Haitian peasant forever looked forward to the day when he could
save enough to buy a pair of shoes. Shoes — and he'd be anybody's equal.

It came to me. This super-Aryan costume of Yole's. His
insistent Americanism. "I'm a Yankee!" over and over again.

Did you ever see a man who was scared he wasn't something try to tell himself that he was? Yole with his flag-waving swagger and clothes overdoing the thing, trying to convince himself.

And other things. His familiarity with native lore. The ease with which he spoke creole dialects. Where had he come from? The consul had told me Yole had been around the islands as long as he could remember. His dark eyes and hair. The look on his face when he'd heard the drums. Touched with fever? Maybe the fever wasn't the only thing poor Yole was touched with.

Well, it gave me something to wonder about. I beat him back to the bungalow; heard him come stumbling in and fall asleep. I wondered all next morning. Yole was packed to go, and, brash as ever, trading with the natives at our office.

But then, just at noon, something happened to make me forget the weird show of the night before. Something happened that wasn't on the books. I'd gone up to the bungalow for lunch; and Yole came bellowing up from the office like a wild bull on the loose. His face was sopping, but it seemed it wasn't from the heat.

"McCord!" he shouted.

Dashing across the floor, he dumped a little fistful of yellow granules on the table.

"Look at this! Just look at this gold!"

He hadn't bothered to undress after his night in the club, and cut an odd figure just then in his incongruous get-up and that derby. I glared at the little mound of gold in some surprise. A pile of tiny nuggets.

"But it's the same stuff that old native up at Morne Lune has been sending down twice a month," I reminded Yole. "What's the matter with it?"

He held out a yellow sliver on his palm. "We thought it was just panning that bird had washed up somewhere," he panted. "It isn't! McCord, you know what that old baboon has been sending us? Coins! Coins chopped into nuggets. Ground up so's we couldn't tell what they were. But this morning he let a piece slip through that's bigger than the others. Know what it is?

It's a hunk chopped from a double doubloon! A Spanish doubloon, dated 1794. He's been chopping up pieces of eight! And there's only one place in Haiti these coins can come from, McCord!" Yole's eyes were dilated. His voice dropped an octave on the words. *"The Voodoo Express!"*

Now there was something! You couldn't go through the West Indies without hearing that Haitian legend at least once, and you heard it more often in Haiti. True, Haiti had more legends per square inch than any other island in the universe, and bigger and better ones, too. There were two kinds, generally speaking. The first had to do with pirate loot, buried treasure; offshoots of the old Spanish Main days when buccaneers were always running around from Santo Domingo to hide out in Haiti's cove-slotted coasts. Buried gold. Yes, and Henri Christophe, the Black King who shot himself with a golden bullet and built that mysterious big castle above Cap Haiti made more color for these yarns, too.

The second class of legend was not so pleasant. This kind generally dealt with primitive superstition, sorcery and voodoo of a pretty woozy nature. While our early Pennsylvania Dutch believed in *hex* and the backwoods Gumbo Ya-Ya Cajuns of Louisiana have all kinds of fetishes and charms, the Caribbean creoles have this black-magic witchcraft called *obeah.* Haiti reeks with that sort of business. Ghosts. Haunts. The Haitians have their own special version. You know about *zombies.* The "undead dead" they call them. Corpses who've been dug up and set to work like mechanical slaves. There are some funny things in Haiti, don't forget it. You can look in Haitian law books right now and see strict warnings forbidding the natives to fool with graves.

Well, there were those two kinds of legendry, and the Voodoo Express business incorporated both of them. I supposed it was only a Haitian variation of the "Flying Dutchman" yarn, but it passed the Dutchman at the halfway mark and left it sinking behind. It started with that old pirate Black-Flag Sebastian who was supposed to have cruised the Haitian coast in the days of cutlass and plank-walking. According to the story, old Black-

Flag got his hooks on a Spanish craft bound for Cuba, and captured a mess of brand new doubloons, the kind that pictured the head of Charles IV, dated 1794, just out of the mint. Then old Black-Flag buried this gold somewhere in Haiti.

Fortune hunters sought after this bonanza for many years and nobody found the treasure, as was usual. Meantime Haiti, a one-time slave colony of France, won freedom under the great black General Toussaint L'Overture, the first military opponent to beat the forces of Napoleon Bonaparte. Later Dessalines ordered every white man on the island put to death. Henri Christophe had set up the Empire of Blacks. The empire had become a republic, and there'd been one president after another with some fierce revolutions in between. Along about 1880 there was another revolution, headed by a creole general named Ti Pierre. Ti Pierre had been quite a man for his time, a big sugar planter. Owned lumber, too. He'd gone to the States and bought himself some books, and he ended up by building thirty miles of railroad track up on Morne Lune. A little railroad running from his lumber mills to his plantation on the coast.

This railroad boasted only one track and one train, but it was an achievement for Haiti. I guess Ti Pierre thought he was smart enough to be president by this time, what with a railroad going for him. So he lit some political firecrackers and started things banging. The Haitian government rushed an army to Morne Lune and licked the stuffing out of Ti Pierre and his army. They bottled him up on the mountain with his railroad, and closed in.

Now, it took money to start a revolution and pay an army even in those days, and the Haitians discovered Ti Pierre had been paying off his troops with Spanish pieces of eight. Somewhere he'd dug up old Black-Flag's 1794 doubloons. Well, the government captured the railroad, track, train and all. Old Ti Pierre, himself, was driving the engine, trying to crash through to the coast. He was killed in the battle, all his men were slain, and the government soldiers smartly reasoned that the doubloons must be somewhere on the train. But the doubloons were never found, and that particular revolution was over.

Do you think the natives on Moon Mountain were going to let a story like that die out? Then you don't know the Haitian mind. That trainload of gold, any mountain native would tell you, still ran down that track. Every night it made the run. There were those who had heard the train whistle as it breezed along. Like Nashville convicts still hear Old 999 in those songs about Birmingham Jail. And in certain phases of the moon, if a man was there at midnight and had sharp eyes, he could see the old express train thunder past.

A white man might say it was the whistle of the wind in the gorge where the train tracks ran, but a white man has poor ears. A white man would think it was thunder on the cliff instead of galloping iron wheels, but a white man didn't know. The Voodoo Express made its phantom midnight run; and what was more, there were dead men working the throttle. There were Ti Pierre's dead soldiers counting the gold in the express cars. A *zombie* fired the engine; and the zombie that was Ti Pierre, himself, the living-dead general, ruled the roost in the locomotive cab. That was the Voodoo Express.

Well, there was your typical Haitian-creole legend; and the fact that it was founded on a certain fragment of truth, the fact that Black-Flag Sebastian had buried some 1794 doubloons around somewhere in 1794, and there had been a Ti Pierre with his railroad and revolution in 1880, didn't make it any more convincing. The fact that every native around Cap Hatien, which was in the Morne Lune region, claimed to have seen the midnight ghost express with the gold-loaded car and *zombie* crew made it less convincing.

But now Conrad Yole stood in the middle of the floor with sweat leaking down his jaw, and the sunshine gleaming on the yellow sliver of minted gold in his palm.

"A chunk from a Spanish doubloon!" he panted. "You can see the date. 1794. McCord, that old crow up at Morne Lune has found that treasure. There's a king's ransom up there, man! A fortune. Quick! That bird just left Cap Haitien for the hills. Come on! We'll trail him! He's found the Voodoo Express!"

CHAPTER II

Twice a month this old mountaineer had been coming to town with his little handful of gold. We called him the Man in the Moon; his right name was Bombier. Every once in a while the hill natives would try washing gold from the creeks; and as Bombier had only been bringing in about twenty dollars' worth at a time, enough to buy himself a few bolts of cloth, a keg of rum or a crate of hens, I hadn't paid him much attention, figuring he was doing a lot of hard placer mining somewhere and his claim would soon peter out. Certainly he had seemed ordinary enough — an old peasant in a pair of ragged pants and floppy straw hat, his bony feet dangling under the belly of a particularly dilapidated donkey.

But when we tried to catch up with Bombier, he became something more than extraordinary. Under normal circumstances two men on horseback could overtake any Haitian on a burro, for there's nothing quite as lazy as a Haitian Hill Billy on a burro. Bombier was something else.

"We'll hire him to guide us up to his Morne Lune diggings," Yole proposed. "He's got a hut up there somewhere, and he can cook our grub, too. We won't tell him we want that treasure; we'll say we're scouting for mahogany." But it was sundown before we caught up with him.

Bowing and scraping to Yole, the ancient peasant was agreeable enough. He offered us his thatched-roof house and cooked up a big meal. Delicious. But next morning he was gone.

"He stuffed us with all that pork and gumbo to put us to sleep," Yole raged. "We've got to trail him and find out where that gold is. When we find him again we've got to stick to him like a burr to its brother." Finding Bombier in that Morne Lune jungle wilderness was a needle-in-haystack problem, however.

That peasant had made himself invisible. We could spot the tracks of his burro on the trail, but we couldn't catch up with the beast. Old Bombier must have known what was in the wind. Yole insisted the man was racing like a jockey, doubling up one gully and down another, keeping under cover of the bush.

I was getting harder put for explanations. About the middle of the next afternoon I was mopping my face and looking nervously at shadows. We should have sighted the old man long ago. He must have been rubbing Aladdin's wonderful lamp or something, to keep himself out of sight.

The chase began to get on my nerves. A Haitian landscape up there near the Santo Domingan border isn't the world's best place for a game of tag. When the good Lord landscaped Haiti, He went in for variety of the sterner kind. There are mountain ranges and deserts, gorges and chasms too deep to peek down, rushing streams, cliffs, crags of polished glass, empty valleys, gloomy summits, swamps, jungles. That ride across the mountainous hinterland of Haiti took us into the whole variety. And it didn't make for the spice of life, either. In the jungle the trail was stifling, steamy as a hothouse. In the open it was a path across a furnace floor, going up. One mile our horses floundered through mats of vine. Next mile they climbed a stony gorge where the rocks radiated like stoves and the sun poured down rays of liquid fire.

Heat lay on the mountain side like a blanket, and silence blanketed that. Far away we could see little patches of brassy ocean, and behind Cap Haitien the citadel of Henri Christophe was a gray frown floating in wisps of cloud. Citadel and ocean passed out of view, and we were alone in a cul-de-sac of ravines.

Not quite alone. Somewhere up ahead of us that scarecrow was racing his burro. But where? Just around the corner? Every time we spurred around the corner nothing was there save tracks. I didn't like the silence either. And I didn't like the looks of thunderclouds banked in glooming formation behind the peak of the morne.

"Yole," I protested, "we should have come up with Bombier long ago. He's wise to us, Yole; knows we're following him. Now we don't want to be trapped in any mountain storm. I've never been in these hills before, either."

No storm was about to stop Conrad Yole. That boy had his nose scenting boxes overflowing with golden coin. He was sure old Bombier had found the Spanish doubloons, chopped them up and brought them in as gold dust. Shrewd old Bombier hadn't wanted anybody to know he'd discovered a treasure. Yole wanted his hands on that fortune. Besides he wasn't going to let any Haitian outwit him.

"Turn back, McCord? With all that gold staring us in the face? Not on your life!" Yole's brown eyes glowed like lamps. He hadn't stopped to grab a sun helmet. The absurd derby on his head must have been like a stove, and his coat was wet across the shoulder-blades. "I'm going to find that Haitian baboon if it's the last thing I do. Come on, he can't be far by now. This way!"

I rammed down my sun helmet, and followed, hand on my pistol butt. We rode through a dark defile full of green under-brush and twists and turns. We had started to pass things. First, a native hut. Sooty smoke spiralled from the clumsy tin chimney, but the door in the wattle wall was open and nobody was inside. Gave me a clammy feeling that the folks at home had heard us coming, cleared out, and now watched us from behind the *sablier* trees up the hill. Then we passed a horse's skull decorating a post planted at roadside. Yole gave the thing no attention, busy following the fresh burro tracks leading ahead. But I didn't like that horse's skull on a post. The bones were too white in the sunshine.

Farther on we galloped under an ancient kapok tree that spread its huge limbs against the sun. The clouds massing behind the mountain were darkening the day, and the atmosphere seemed to be waiting. And something was waiting in that giant tree. The air on the trail was bad, alive with the buzzing of feasting flies. A shadow fell across the path. I don't know why the goat should have cooled my blood the way it did. But the goat hung by a cord depended from a lower limb of the tree, and flies swarmed at a black gash in the dead animal's throat.

"There!" Yole yelled. "He turned up there! Up the bank of that stream!"

We weren't chasing an old crow on a donkey. We were chasing just donkey tracks. Chasing them across a corner of Haiti where invisible habitants planted horses' skulls at roadside and cut the throats of goats and hung them in roadside trees. Just an old Haitian custom. But it made me think of the gang that had jumped President Sam and chopped him up like Bombier had chopped up those confounded doubloons. I began to look back over my shoulder, wishing it wouldn't get dark. The thunder-heads on the peak had completely stifled the afternoon. Leaves started dropping from trees we'd pass, sifting groundward without a sound. We passed another horse-skull on a post.

"Yole," I protested, "this is nonsense. Bombier can play hide and seek with us all afternoon, and we're going to get caught in a dandy little tempest, by the looks. Besides, the natives may be mighty ugly."

"We're white men, aren't we?" he snarled. "And here's our chance to clean up and skip out of this hell hole. That man has found the pirate gold, I tell you! Gold! Boxes of the stuff! Ti Pierre, the Haitian general, toted it in a train. That damned railroad was somewhere up on this hill. We'll show these Haitians what real men can do, and — "

"But that damned train wouldn't still be there, man!" I snapped. "More than likely the treasure was found years ago. Maybe this Bombier found only a few coins, or — Look, Yole, you don't expect to find that confounded express train?"

"That's a fake Haitian legend, you fool!" He was shaking with impatience, bending in saddle to study the path. "But the gold can still be around somewhere. Doubloons! A fortune. I'm going to find it."

We had reached a clearing. Our horses stood neck to neck. Yole shot a hand to fasten on my wrist. "Look, man! There's the — train tracks!"

There they were. They came out of a fold cleaving the rocks,

curved into a high-banked gully and so on down the mountainside to be lost in a forest of jungle trees. I wonder if you can
imagine how strange they looked, against that background of
wild mountain, bending sharply out of that gully to run across
the clearing, vanish into the jungle, and take us by surprise. I
say the late afternoon sun was darkening, and a shadow loomed
over the world. A zigzag of lightning flickered like a knitting
needle in and out of the clouds banked on the morne. The clouds
grumbled faintly, breathing a wind that puffed dust up the trail
and shook the underbrush.

Yole sat stiff in saddle, derby tilted over his illuminated
eyes, a finger pointing. On the morne there flickered another
zigzag needle. The light brought cliffs into view and the clouds
hunched together and growled. And prickles crawled across my
neck as I stared at those curving tracks. Rusty, brown railroad
tracks, abandoned on a roadbed dim with weeds.

And then I saw something else. Across the tracks a gray
shadow moved behind a banana tree. A burro. I let out a yell,
and Yole hollered, too. That was Bombier's donkey over there,
tied to a post. And that was no ordinary hitching post on the
other side of those tracks. You bet it wasn't. Stuck on the top of
that post was a round, white knob. A human skull!

But Yole was out of his saddle with a whoop. "McCord!
Look! That devil! He ran up the tracks. See where his feet
smashed those weeds! This is Ti Pierre's railroad, McCord!"
Yole wiped his mouth with a sleeve. "And Bombier's gone to
get that gold!"

Yole ran. Stooped low, he followed the rusty tracks up the
slope, disappeared around the bend of the gully. I wasn't going
to be left behind, I can promise you that. Automatic in fist, I
went up the track after him. I was glad when the skull-festooned
post was left behind, but those rusty rails were not much better
than bones. There's something indescribably gloomy about an
abandoned railroad bed. That track on that Haitian mountain
made one think of graves. Weeds tufted the ties. Vines crossed
the corroded rails, and if the gully there hadn't been shored up

by boulders and rocks the jungle would have wiped the roadbed out long before.

I was glad to see that no train had run on those tracks for thirty years at least. That spiked the native legend and that was a comfort. If ever there was a place where an express train could be run by dead men it was down that particular cut in the hills. The canyon was filled with a blue, misty dusk, ghostly with that lull before the storm. Our boots crunched and slipped on the rotted ties.

"We'll catch him!" Yole gasped out. "He can't be far."

Did you ever try to sprint on mossy railway ties? Then you'll know. We were running uphill, too. Up a narrow canyon, high-walled on either side, that curved and twisted like a roller-coaster track in Coney Island. The dusk thickened. High atop the mountain the thunderclouds turned black. A yellow knife stabbed fast across the sky. The clouds boomed. Side by side we rounded a sharp elbow in the track, and there was another noise. *Spang!* The track turned another corner up ahead, and we didn't see the blaze. But Yole's fool derby made a jump to the back of his head. A hole smoked in the derby's crown.

If you think that rifle-shot stopped Conrad Yole, you're wrong. Mad? He didn't have a gun to fire, so he tried a fusillade of oaths. He kept right on running, and picked up speed. He was shouting.

"Bombier did have a gun — I remember! Old LePage smooth-bore. And he'd dared shoot at me, that lousy Haitian! Shoot at an American, will he? I'll break his neck!"

Yole wasn't a coward. There was that hole in his derby. If the light had not been so uncertain it might have been a hole in his head. It made me a little sick. My hand sweat on my gun. We ran up that rotten old railroad track, and a Haitian was waiting around the bend with a rifle. But the Haitian hadn't waited. We charged around the bend and I uncorked a bullet on the turn. And Bombier wasn't there. There was nothing but rusty track, brown ties under ankle-high weeds.

Yole got madder. His boots hammered on the decaying ties.

His coat flagged. He skidded and fell down and bounced up mad as a hatter. Those ties were just the things to skid on, and the roadbed underneath was a masterpiece of sharp stones. I've seen some mean railroad tracks in my day, but never a line to match that one. On the next bend I gave my ankle a scorching twist.

Yole, too, developed a hobble. It was getting him in earnest. Somewhere up the mountain ahead was that old coot with a gun. Anticipation may be better than realization, but it's a mighty nervous feeling. Every bend in that trail might bring a bullet whizzing to knock us kicking in the gloom. I reminded Yole of this.

"You going to let him get away? You going to lose that treasure? Not me! I'll catch that jackal and find that gold no matter what."

It rained. The roar of falling water drowned Yole's words. The sky collapsed with a bang; dropped a blinding flood. Niagara Falls stormed down from the morne. Fountains sprang from the rocks. Black water whirled through the air. A river raced, frothing, down the tracks. Liquid night. Cloudburst torrent. We floundered around a hairpin curve and climbed.

A yard ahead of me Yole disappeared. Livid daylight flashed everywhere and he was a maniac in a derby hat vaulting ties in the rain. Darkness fell with a stunning crash. The mountain trembled under concussion. The sky flashed, crashed, wept and banged. We ran through a torrent of dark water that exploded. Lightning shot a cloud overhead and blew the air to pieces. The joints in the iron tracks crackled; spat sparks. The banks of the canyon quivered. Geysers spouted out of the boulders. We were engulfed. I stumbled in a gutter of ink and then Yole and I were exposed in a flare of white light. A great moment for an enemy gun. You couldn't have seen a powder-flash, puny compared to the explosions in the sky.

Yole stalled with a shout, and grabbed my arm. I stopped with water bucketing down my face. A blue flame licked twice

overhead, and I saw what Yole had to yell about. That railroad track wasn't running through a canyon here. It was running along the rim of one. On the far side a cliff went up to the sky. On our side the mountain dropped off. With a drop to freeze your marrow.

We ran along the edge of the drop, following the track. Lightning flared, and I saw a curve. We rounded a corner of granite and went through a grove of thorny *sablier* trees. Remember, we were running the ties in the teeth of a mountain storm, and ahead of us was a man with a gun.

Yole yelled again and we were on the edge of a deeper chasm. The rusty rails curved along this chasm-ring, and a three-second display of terrific chain-lightning lit up the picture. That chasm must have dropped a quarter mile. Looking down, I saw a flat floor of yellow sand far below. It was a long way down.

After that I didn't look down. I watched Yole jump in and out of darkness, and tried to keep up with him and stay away from that awful ledge. A quarter mile farther on, we were in a forest of giant palms. No sign of Bombier. I hoped he had given up the race, maybe slipped away in the jungle. Then Yole found the print of a naked heel, and we kept going.

The mountainside howled with rain. Thunder sounded like cannon. Yole vanished in the noise and water. Suddenly I heard him scream. He gave a loud scream to be heard above that tempest, I can tell you. And he had a strong reason to scream, take my word. "Stop!" he screamed; and in a blast of lightning I saw him pitch to his face. I pitched to my own face, let me tell you. At that very instant the rain stopped. The rain stopped and the lightning stopped and a hole appeared by magic across the sky to let a stormy sunset-light streak across the world. You know how tropic thunderstorms come to a dead end? That storm came to a dead end then and there, and so did the forest of palms.

And there in front of us dropped a chasm that beat all the chasms in the world. The mountain sheared right off and fell away in front of our rattling chins. We were sprawling on the edge of a cliff that dropped into infinity. The sunset light fell down and down and down that canyon, and away at the bottom a creek was like a tiny thread of blood. My fingers clawed the mud under me to keep hold. A stone rattled out from under my hand and vanished in that awful depth. And the sweat bubbled out on my face. It was a trestle that did it. A railway trestle spanning that gulf! That wrung the sweat out of me.

I take off my hat to that Haitian, Ti Pierre. He must have been a genius, indeed, to get engineers who would build a trestle across that slice in the world. There it was. A wooden bridge crossing the gulf. It was only two hundred feet across? Yes, but it was two hundred miles when you consider the depth below. A narrow wooden span just wide enough for the iron rails and the ties. There it hung. A spidery thread suspended in mid-air. Vines dangled from the rotted timbers. Moss dripped from the ties. And in one place three ties were gone. Near the middle. The ties were gone like missing teeth. Leaving just two iron rails like strings of rust in the air.

I guess my jaw wasn't doing a dance! Another step and I'd have stumbled out on that trestle. It would have taken nerve in the daylight. What wouldn't it have been like in that inky tempest? The next puff of wind would send the thing crashing, by the looks. And there was that hole in the middle. Whew! The sky opened up to let crimson twilight wash down the mountain, and I lay on my stomach and groaned. Looking over the void, I glared at the iron rails where there weren't any ties. On the other rim of the chasm the tracks disappeared into a tunnel in the mountain wall. A picture to hang in the office of some tour agency, but as far as I was concerned, that was it. I wasn't going to try to cross that trestle in the twilight. Not me! I glared at Yole. He was belly-to-mud beside me, and something to look at with that punctured derby tilted over his twisted face. There wasn't a sound to be heard save the dripping jungle foliage behind us, the burble of rain water draining off into the brush.

Yole was panting, his eyes fixed on the mouth of the tunnel across the chasm.

Somewhere a parakeet squawked. I opened my mouth to curse. And a voice behind me said in a melodeous creole accent, "Good evening. Are you waiting for the train?"

CHAPTER III

"Good evening. Are you waiting for the train?"

The sort of nice little speech a kindly conductor with a watch in his hand might use in interrogating a yokel couple sitting in a rural depot. But Yole and I, bounding up out of the mud with a concert holler and pivoting around on the rim of that gulf, weren't an old couple. We weren't in any rural depot, either. we were on a wilderness mountain in Haiti, standing in the middle of an impossible railroad track that climbed out of sunset-reddened palms, swooped across a canyon too deep to spit down, and vanished into a black hole in the opposite cliff. And the man who interrogated us was nobody's kindly conductor! I hope to tell you. Holy cow! He wasn't even a man!

Haiti was a queer place in those days. A tropical Eden in the Caribbean trying to be a republic. But the laws of a republic didn't flourish there any more than they did in the Garden of Eden. There's a law against voodoo, but it worked about as well as prohibition did in Chicago. They bootlegged voodoo in the Haitian mountains bordering Santo Domingo the way liquor was bootlegged on the Canadian border. And this creature confronting Yole and me that evening was the Al Capone of all voodoo bootleggers. If ever I saw a load of Haitian voodoo, I saw it standing there smiling at me.

Give your imagination a shot of hasheesh and try to see the picture. try to see the character who asked us if we waited for the train. There he stood under a dripping tree, bare feet in a pond of sunset light. A Congo witch doctor. Broad shoulders. Powerful arms. Large white-gloved hands. You know those brass-buttoned coats London doormen wear? God knows where

99

he'd won such a coat, or the fancy brown tophat with the feather in its band to go with it. The topper was jaunty on his bullet-shaped head, and the dress coat was a phantasy on his shoulders. That specimen came bowing straight out of a Mississippi Show Boat minstrel show, except for his skirt. I mean he wore a dress! Instead of trousers, he had on a flouncy white petticoat with fancy lace tickling his ankle bones.

He hadn't stopped there. Under one arm he carried a Haitian voodoo drum — one of those shell-shaped tom-toms with a goatskin head. Under his other arm was a dead rooster. A belt of coconut rattles and bones and gourds encircled his waist, and a human jawbone hung from a necklace of teeth about his throat. Pretty jewelry to set off a prettier face. For the cheeks were rosy-black satin dimpling above a broad inviting smile. His eyes were bulbous bird's-eggs with little hammocks swung underneath. And those bulging eyes with hammocks under them were screened by enormous sun-glasses of tinted glass.

Maybe you think that wasn't a costume to jolt your spine! The sunset gleamed on those goggles and made of them eclipsed moons. The face under the jaunty plug hat smiled that cordial smile. I stared at the lace petticoat, dead rooster and drum, and cold things crawled up and down my skin. I knew what those dark glasses and that lace petticoat meant. The goggles were symbolic of the blindness of corpses. The skirt symbolized a burial robe. This man was a high priest of the dreaded Culte des Mortes; master of Petro and Legba rituals — the weirdest of all Haitian creole voodoo. A *papaloi* witch-doctor; half man, half woman; Oracle of Death.

There was that molasses voice again.

"Are you waiting for the train?"

This time the question entered my head by way of my hair-roots, and every hair went stiff. Were we waiting for the train? The words carried a startling implication; they implied that a train might come! I glared at Conrad Yole. Sundown painted red shadows on his face, and his eyes had narrowed with anger. Making angry fists, he took a step toward the grinning Haitian.

"Look here, you walking sideshow. What do you mean? And what you doing sneaking up behind us like this? Where'd you come from?"

The fat cheeks dimpled. "Your pardon, *monsieur*. I am Papa Gobo, high priest of this Mountain of the Moon. My *houmfort*, where the sacred *rada* drums and the soul of Damballa are enshrined, is not far distant on the mountain peak. I have only just come from the coast where three *zombies* were held in the power of a wicked sugar planter and calling for my charms to release them back to their graves."

My scalp crawled. I had heard of *houmforts* — temples of voodoo where all manner of un-Christian doings went on. *Rada* drums were the choicest of Haitian tom-toms, and Damballa was the African snake-god responsible, so the natives said, for turning men into goats. And this scoundrel with his sun glasses and dead rooster was talking of his ministry with corpses.

"Can the rot!" Yole snapped. "Tell us what you want."

"But to warn you, *messieurs*," the apparition wheedled. "Only to warn you. I was but coming up the trail in the storm when I thought I heard the sound of the white man's gun. Thunder speaks with one tongue; the firearm with another. I saw you running up this track, and I saw you fall as in prayer. It is no night to run on this track, my white friends. For the train, *messieurs*, the train of Ti Pierre — "

Yole roared, and got a clutch on that witch doctor's arm.

"Stow the bunk, you snakehead-eater, and save it for your barefoot, drum-knocking believers! Speak up, then get the hell out of here. Fast, before I bust those glasses off your nose! Did you see anybody else on this track? Did a little old *salopard* with a rifle come dodging up these rails? Did he cross that trestle?"

Yole pointed to the tottering span at the tunnel-mouth across the chasm. The witch doctor grinned.

"Papa Gobo saw nobody else, *monsieur!* No inhabitant of these mountains ever crosses that bridge. No, no! The bridge is sacred to us, *messieurs*, and feared. For who knows at what time the train will come?"

It got to Yole. The twilight and the dripping jungle, the dead rooster, jawbone and all the rest of that flaky Haitian atmosphere. There was a luster in Yole's eyes that didn't belong there, and the whole business was getting woozy as a séance in a quack clairvoyant's parlor.

"I suppose," I jibed at our professor of voodoo, "that your railroad doesn't run to schedule, eh? The old engineer, Casey at the throttle, whoops up a lot of ghost steam and comes down the line any minute, right? And that rooster under your arm is beginning to smell." I turned on Yole. "Come on," I urged, "let's clear out. Old Bombier's given us the slip. He may be up there drawing a bead on us right now. He didn't cross that trestle, and he's not going to. It'll be dark in a minute, and we've got to look to our mounts. As for the gold — "

As for the gold! I shouldn't have mentioned it.

"The gold," said the creature in the topper and skirt, "will be on the train when it comes. The gold that Ti Pierre was trying to escape with. But no man shall touch the gold, for the dead who guard it shall guard it forever, even as the train shall run forever."

And then he was telling us the story of the Voodoo Express. Man! How that old devil could tell a story! Five times I opened my mouth to tell Yole we had to start out of there, but I couldn't interrupt that voice. The witch-doctor had a wizard's technique. He had genius. He had a voice and a delivery that had all the spell-binders and silver-tongued orators of the past and present backed off the map. That Haitian pitch-man had all the midway tricks and a few more of his own invention.

His voice went up to falsetto to make you cry; it dropped to deep bass to make your finger-tips prickle. It crooned and chanted, whispered and droned. It sent the sun flaming down behind Morne Lune and developed a red moon round as a dollar, and hung it up in the sky. It blacked out the canyons in shadows and brought purple gloom flooding through the jungle. That *papaloi* cast a spell.

Like wooden cigar-store Indians, Yole and I stood there;

and that wretched Haitian squatted in a pool of moonlight, rooster and drum fixed between his knees, mesmerizing us. The rising moon was mirrored in his goggles, like glowing eyeballs in each cloudy glass. The white gloves waved and gesticulated. Those hands! They were pickpockets stealing your brains.

Speak of prestidigitation! He could do more tricks with those white-glove hands than were ever done by Harry Houdini or Thurston the Great. His fingers made butterflies fluttering before our eyes. With his voice they pianoed up and down the scale. They wigwagged deaf-and-dumb alphabets. They performed little pantomimes — this-is-the-church, this-is-the-steeple. They made puppet faces. Genuflected. Beckoned. Danced. You couldn't take your eyes off those agile, capering fingers. Finally they wove an invisible hangman's noose that I could literally feel around my neck. And that jungle sorceror came to the finale of his voodoo pitch. He began to caress the drum head.

Listen! He made us see that story. He made us visualize old Ti Pierre with his soldiers and trainload of ancient Spanish gold. He made us see the government troops creeping up the mountain with moonlight on their guns, the scouts with knives and pistols, the black generals with their swords. Those generals of the government were powerful. Ti Pierre was caught in a trap. His train was stopped somewhere on the other side of that chasm. He and his men were killed.

They killed many government troops, though. The gods of Haiti were angry at the revolutionists. Old Ti Pierre hadn't paid his dues to the voodo doctors. The gods of Legba and Petro revenged themselves on Ti Pierre. He had sneered at them and played with a foreign imperialistic toy. Therefore he and his men should be dead but yet alive. No rest in the grave for them. They could run their foreign train, world without end. And every night the train with its crew of living corpses would make its grisly run.

When he narrated the battle-scenes the witch doctor thumbed his drum, and we heard the mutter of muskets. When he told of the train and its *zombie* crew the witch doctor pounded the drum head, and we heard the ghostly gallopy-gallop of engine and cars. He breathed through his teeth, and the train was whistling. He wheezed, and we heard the locomotive valves steam.

"The dead men!" he intoned. "Their white faces peek out of the cars. Their blue hands are counting the gold. The engine goes by like a wind in the dark. And when the moon is full like it is tonight — "

"Stop it!"

Yole yelled to yank us back into reality. I tell you, the man was a raw nerve. His face was screwed up as if he was going to cry. His teeth gritted. He held a fist like a white stone waving up over his derby.

"You infernal jackal!" he shouted at the witch doctor. A light of panic dilated his brown eyes, and he seemed to notice for the first time that it had grown dark. "You've told us lies to keep us standing here so's that devil Bombier could sneak off with the gold. You lie! It's a lie, McCord!" The man was beside himself. "Come on! There's no such thing as a train run by dead men. Let's go across!"

"Listen!"

The Haitian priest whirled the dead rooster and flung it to the stars. His cry smacked Yole into stone; turned my feet into blocks of ice. For the night was suddenly shaken by a strange, echoic rumbling that grew louder and louder in the moonlit gloom. The ground shivered under my boots. A sword of pale lightning lashed twice across the sky behind the peak. The earth beneath me heaved. Pebbles went rattling down into the dark-smothered chasm and palms showered from the trees. The shocks of a brief earthquake.

Then Witch Doctor Gobo was pointing at the tunnel mouth at the far end of the trestle. Yole and I went pop-eyed. The noise became a queer, rackety banging. Abruptly it was muffled to an undertone, subterranean whiskey-whish, whiskety-wish, like the rapid beat of a jazz drummer's whiskbroom on cymbals. Then a long-drawn whoo-whoo-whoeeee burst from the mouth of the tunnel. The witch doctor yowled. I howled. Yole screamed.

"The Voodoo Express!"

Can you hear the train blow? That whistle-blast went trailing down the canyon with an echo that wakes me out of nightmares today.

And out of the tunnel's black maw charged a swaying locomotive and ghostly string of cars.

CHAPTER IV

How can I tell it? How can I describe that rust-eaten engine, that battered tender and trio of antiquated express cars that came blowing and swinging from that black tunnel, swerved out on the tottering trestle, and swept down on us like a banging, clanging apparition.

The sight paralyzed me for a moment. WOW! A bath of red moonlight flooding down from the sky washed the night with somber color. Bathed in a phantom glow, that train was the stuff of dreams. My hair stood at attention.

A train coming head-on down the track is always a thriller. Talk about the Empire State Express. Twentieth Century Limited. Chicago Wolverine. Today's Super Chief. Yesterday's Black Diamond. The old Phoebe Snow. Or the beloved Chattanooga Choo-choo, if you will. None of them could hold a candle to this Haitian Flyer. Undoubtedly it took first prize.

An old locomotive of the Civil War type, wheeling straight out of the past. It rushed straight at us out of a vanished yesterday, with its fan-top smoke-stack, its square headlamp like a dead eye set above the smoke box, its long-nosed cowcatcher. No plume of smoke streamed from the swinging stack. No steam blew from piston cylinders and valve heads. The driving arms were like skeleton elbows, old bones that moved of their own accord. Rusty axles squealed behind the drive wheels. Greaseless couplers cried out. Iron links clanged. And just as the train hit the trestle the bell behind the stack started a phantom bonging, unreal as tolling in a tomb.

Clanking, clattering, rattling in every bolt, that train came on like an iron Zombie. Talk about the living dead! That en-

gine, itself, was a dead thing with life, resurrected from its locomotive graveyard to run the tracks without steam. Flakes of rust
flew from its flanged wheels. Ribbons of vine trailed like tat-
tered green flags from the handrails above the rotted running
boards. In the phantasmal moonlight the wet, rusty iron resembled metal eaten with old bloodstain. And I tell you that
headlamp rushing at us was a cyclopean dead eye — a blind,
dead eye sheathed by a cataract of ghostly cobwebbing.

Rocking like a ship in high seas, the train slammed out on
the trestle. And that trestle swayed. Speed. That is what got the
express across. Fifty miles an hour on the down grade. That
rusty, clanking dream-train was moving, I tell you! The rotten
trestle didn't have time to collapse. The timbers shrieked out
loud under screaming trucks — but this was Haiti. The skeleton
stood up for the skeleton. The train made it.

"Jump!" I howled.

I had to hit Yole to move him. He was standing on the track
like an image. I whaled him hard on the back, and he went spinning into the open-mouthed voodoo doctor, and we tangled,
getting off just in time. The engine pounded by with drivers
hammering. I caught a brief vision of rusty wheels and fast-
cranking arms as it leaned over in passing.

A loose chain whipped out from somewhere and missed
my nose by an inch. Somewhere in that jangle of grinding, ban-
shee machinery a bolt snapped off and shot past my head like
a bullet. The engine flew by. I'm not lying. The wheels pounded
right past my face.

And then I saw something that took off my scalp and hung
it six inches above my head. An arm. An arm hanging from the
cab window. An arm of white bones in a sleeve of rotted cloth
with a greasy gauntlet swinging at its end. I couldn't see the
engineer. He'd slipped down somewhere inside, thank God.
But the gauntlet waved as the engine shot buy, and I yelled with
a mouth full of dough.

Can you see that train, that impossible, preposterous lim-

ited rocking past through the gloom? Clanking and groaning and pounding into the moonlit palm forest, leaning over like a drunk on the curve? Can you see the three of us crouching like tramps beside the track? Mighty weird tramps, let me tell you; me with my mouth like an opened trapdoor; Yole with eyes popping under the rim of his derby; and that Papa Gobo, looking pretty green around the gills with his plug hat and lace skirt and bulging goggles — looking, come to think of it, a little like a magician whose conjuring had got out of control, and, instead of a rabbit, had produced from his handkerchief an elephant.

Well, I yelled. Papa Gobo did some shrill yelling, too. I don't know what Conrad Yole did as the three ancient and stale express cars clanked past. But just as the last car careened by — and I'll never forget how that car's rear door was open and banging back and forth like a shutter in a haunted house — Yole did something that made me yell again and twice as loud. The engine must have slowed a trifle on an upgrade, for Conrad Yole made a flying leap and caught the back platform of that last car.

Heaven knows what moved my own rubbery legs. I know I didn't. Was a time when I could hop a train with the best of them; and only subconscious, practiced feet got me aboard that platform with Yole. I didn't want to be there, but there I was. Papa Gobo was there, too. I suppose he found some bat wings somewhere and flew through the air. I caught a glimpse of his skirt umbrellaing in the wind as he clung on the bottom steps and we hit a curve; and then he was leaning against me, and I had my automatic clutched for comfort in my hand.

The Voodoo Express went rocking through the black jungle, and we were passengers on the train.

"Come on!" Yole yelled at me. "I'm going in."

I expected to wake up in bed when he put a hand on the door and balanced on that rocking platform. But the door didn't fade from view as doors do in decent nightmares. Yole disappeared in the inner darkness. Icicles oozed out of my pores. My left hand, clamped on the platform rail, didn't want to let go. That train had only slowed for a minute; now it was hammering down the track like the Twentieth Century two hours late. And rocking? Wow! Those cars were tipping from side to side like boats in a hurricane. Maybe you think I wasn't hanging on. I didn't want to go after Yole. My Colt .45 wasn't any comfort at all in this situation.

"Come back!" I bawled at Yole. "Come back, you crazy fool! We've got to get off!"

A wild laugh was all that came back through the slamming door. The train careened around a curve, flung me against the jabbering witch doctor, and we almost toppled off the platform. Cursing, I shoved myself free of the tangle of drum, arms, top hat and lace dress; balanced a moment, and watched trees whiz by. I told you that track was like a Coney Island roller-coaster. All downhill, and some of the wildest curves in any railroad. And when I thought of those old ties crumbling under us, those old rusted rails spread at the joints, and lacking spikes, ice water poured down my forehead.

"She's running away!" I howled at the door where Yole had gone.

That didn't stop her for a minute. Or him. We hit another curve, and the trucks made a racket like a thousand wheels in a switch-yard. Papa Gobo hung beside me clutching his drum, his dress flagging like a distress signal.

I gave him a push in the face, and grabbed the iron ladder going up to a hand brake atop the car. There was just enough of the red moonlight to see by. Just enough to see how dangerous it was. A boomer walking the deck of a fast freight in a hurricane would have had a picnic compared to my clamber up that rusty ladder. Lady Luck certainly hoisted me up to the top of that lurching express car. And then she abandoned me there.

I didn't have a club to ram into the spokes of that hand-brake wheel, and it wouldn't have done me any good if I'd had. I got a clutch on that wheel like the grip of Death; yanked at the rim with all my might. It turned, all right. It turned in my hand,

and pulled around. And twisted with a snap and broke clean away. And there I clung on that swaying ladder, clutching a rusty iron wheel connected to nothing.

Anyway, the brakes on that train would've been about as strong as wet tissues. The axles under the cars were squealing louder at every wheel-turn. I remember getting down to the platform and clinging there just hollering as we sped on through the downhill jungle like nothing on earth, and surely nothing in heaven. The trees were flickering by like movie film unwinding in bad light. *Whizz!* and another stretch of track vanished astern. The moon was like a red wafer in the velvet sky behind the trees, and it jumped all over the heavens — now here, now there — as the train shot around the sharp curves.

"Yole!" I screeched. "Yole!" Once more his laugh echoed out of the car. *Clickety-clack, clank-bang,* we sped down the track; and I made a grab for the swinging door and got through. The minute I got in there I was sorry. The light was too dim. The floor lifted under me, flung me against a wall. I rapped my head against something plenty hard, and came up jittering with my face swathed in cobwebs. Yole wasn't there. The only thing in that car was what was left of me, what was left of three oil lamps that swung wildly under the ceiling, and what was left of four skeletal mummies that slid back and forth across the floor at the other end. Not Egyptian mummies! I mean Haitian mummies! Bony corpses with skulls the color of tobacco. Clad in uniforms that once must have been as gaudy as cigar-bands, but now were tatters and shreds.

Yole had gone into the car up ahead. What a maniac. I danced past the mummies and got into the second car just in time to see Yole going into the car behind the tender. The floor jumped under me in a violent pitch and sent me reeling down another aisle draped with cobwebs. In the dark that train seemed to be going faster than ever. Another mummy slithered on the beastly floor, and an iron thing gave a jump past my toes — an old-fashioned horse-pistol. The car rolled from side to side, and the mummy tagged me, and I hollered to heaven and bounded for the car behind the tender.

Yole was in there, battling at a jammed door. When I wailed at him he flung around.

"The gold, you fool! It's got to be somewhere aboard. Come on!"

Just then we took a curve; and the handle came off the door to let it whip open; and Yole was scrambling up the tender's stern with a whoop. I want to tell you that tender was swaying. Yole hung on for dear life at the top of the ladder, and I hung on with him. There we hung; wind lashing our cheeks; the car bumping and jolting and rocking; our ears deaf with the noise of shrieking irons and galloping wheels. We hung there, you understand, on the slanting stern of the tender. We went no farther. The tender wasn't full of coal, that's why. It was full of something else. The bunker in front of us was alive with snakes!

Snakes? That tender was a hive of them. A breeding place for half the snakes of Haiti. Big snakes and little snakes, fat snakes and lanky snakes were coiled and tangled in one frantic, hissing, poisonous stew in the bunker before us. They were rabid mad, too. I suppose they'd been living in the water compartment and having a grand time till their world started moving at fifty miles an hour through the dark. Now they whipped and lashed around in the open bunker like colored ropes, shooting their flat heads up at the sky and sticking out their tongues. If there was one snake on board, there were five hundred.

"My God!" Yole squawked, pointing. Not at the snakes. I'd already noticed them and put them down in my memory book. But he pointed at the engine-cab up ahead. Can you guess what he was pointing at? I'll tell you, for I saw it close-up.

The moon was behind us, and that locomotive cab was full of a witchy light. The cab swayed from side to side — I can still hear that bell's ghostly tolling — and there in the driver's seat sat a man. Not the one with his arm waving out of the window. That was on the opposite seat. This hogger of an engineer lounged on the side-seat, for all the world like Dan Rooney of the Empire State wheeling her west of Syracuse, save that his feet were askew, his hand looked loose on the throttle, his head wagged crookedly on his neck, and a little green snake hung from the hip pocket of his pants. The cab gave a lurch; the engineer lurched; Yole and I lurched as we went lickety-split around another hairpin curve.

Before Yole or I could collect some wits, we hit another curve with a tilt to curl your hair; and my hair did curl. Lord! That engineer slithered up out of his seat, gave a half turn, screwed around to look at us and give us a look at his face. His hands let go of the throttle; and he came toward us with a grimace. He was the deadest engineer I'd ever seen.

You'll say it was the roll of the curve that threw him up off his seat and swung him around to walk him toward us. And probably he didn't get very far. All right. But you'd have said differently had you been there with us at the time. You wouldn't have waited to see how far he walked. A dead engineer running a dead locomotive; firing the dead furnace with snakes! And then to have him swing around to stare at you with his sightless eyes —

Yole's cry in the night was that of a tortured soul; and he acrobated down that tender's stern like someone gone batty in a circus. I wasn't so slow, myself. I joined him in a race through the darkness where mummies rolled on the floor. We didn't dilly-dally. We covered the length of that train in nothing flat.

In the last car Yole went into a somersault that carried him out to the platform and wrapped him around the witch doctor there. Stubbing a boot, I dived into the tangle. the train swerved drunkenly on a curve; racketed across a stretch of field to leave the jungle behind; and the witch doctor, Yole and I went spilling off the platform in a triple somersault.

We must have rolled sixty feet on the ground, but we sat up in time to see that last car with its banging door vanish around a bend.

I remember our witch doctor hugging his drum, his plug hat pushed down over his ears, his goggles askew, his face squeezed out of shape. Yole squatted in a mess of plantain, derby on the back of his head, blood leaking from a gash in his chin, eyes on something in his palm.

I watched that train go out of sight; then I concentrated on the thing in Yole's palm. His eyes bugged at it. So did mine. But his were too buggy, if you know what I mean. That thing in his palm was a gold coin. He didn't need to tell me it happened to be a Spanish doubloon. A double doubloon!

Yole leapt to his feet with his loudest shout of the evening. "Look at this, McCord! It came out of one of those cars. I must have grabbed it up when I fell!" His voice went hoarse. "Let's go! There's gold on that express!"

My voice wasn't hoarse. "Are you completely nuts? How the devil can we overtake that runaway train?"

His arms semaphored. "That long hairpin turn half way down the morne. At least ten miles by the railroad. We can short-cut down this canyon wall and grab the train below here. Run!"

He had lost his mind? So had I. We plunged down the wall of the canyon, grabbing at handholds in the underbrush. The good witch doctor accompanied us. Yole wanted to beat the iron horse by cutting across the jungle racetrack. I wanted to see him do it. And Papa Gobo wanted to keep up with the betting.

Time-wise, we beat the odds, too. We sprinted down a steep grade, crossed a creek, crashed through brush, clawed down-hill through a grove of *sablier* trees, and stumbled out onto a ridge where the railroad tracks came around the bend. Yole bounded down to the roadbed, blattering.

"It hasn't come yet! The weeds haven't been disturbed! Get set to hop aboard!"

Maybe Yole was ready to hop. I know I sat down on a rock and uttered some of the best oaths in my vocabulary. The doctor sat down beside me, hugging his drum. We waited. I was getting my breath back, and some of my brain. We waited some more. Yole waited too. We craned there in the moonlight, our eyes nailed on the bend in the canyon around which the train should come. This time we were really waiting for that train.

Well, two minutes ticked by, and something told me that

train should have been along then and there. Another minute ticked by. The train was late. Five minutes. Ten minutes. No train. I wish you could have seen Yole's face.

"Now!" he danced on his toes. "Here it comes! Listen!"

But it was only the wind on the morne.

"Here it comes now!"

But it was only a gust in the *sablier* trees.

Do you get the scene? That cursed engine and cars should have clanked into view by that time at the latest. And? No. Nothing.

Now I'll tell you something. I hated that train like the devil. Yet, by heaven, I wanted that iron horse to come clattering around that bend like I never wanted anything before. I wanted to be sure that it was really a train we had caught and not some ghostly horror from Hades.

I watched that curve in the track with every nerve straining beneath my skin. I begged at the track. No, sir, that confounded train hadn't gone by, but the time ticked away and it didn't arrive. No sound of hammering pistons. No Chattanooga Choo-Choo whistle. Only a stillness like deafness came around the bend. No train.

The hush in that scene became oppressive. Silence and moonlight and a stretch of rusty track. If that train didn't come in another minute I was going to explode like a lot of smashed springs. No. All that came around that bend was the terminal silence of a cemetery. And longer shadows as the moon cruised down.

I glared at Yole. His face had turned grotesque, chalky. At the witch doctor. What do you think that gentleman was doing? He was smiling! Once more the smoky goggles were the symbols of death, the ebony cheeks were dimpling, and the lips curved upward in a sweet all-knowing smile. And then I went up like so much TNT!

I don't quite remember what I said. I'll bet my life it was profane! And I don't quite remember how I got there, but there I went legging it up that frowsty railroad track and around the

canyon bend, looking for an engine, a tender and three cars.
Looking for three express cars where mummies tumbled in
the dark, and for a rusty, old fan-stack engine with a dead engineer lounging in the cab.

Just to help me out the moon dodged into a nest of smoky
green clouds and the landscape retired in blue shadows. Just to
help me out some more, the track reeled along the edge of a
cliff, leaving no place to jump if that express did come. A steep
wall of rock on one side, chasm on the other. Where could an
engine, a tender and three old cars on a single track have gone?
This wasn't the Main Line of the New York Central with accom-
modations for the Broadway Limited. What had happened to
that Morne Lune special coming down a single track? Maybe
you think I didn't want to know? How could an old dead locomotive and three decaying cars play hide and seek with me on
that mountainside?

I came to that curve along the rim of a cliff, and I peered
down over the edge. No train in view. Nothing save that flat
sweep of bare sand. I fled on up into a canyon, close-walled on
either side. The train was nowhere to be seen. I ran like the
devil. I ran all the way up that impossible mountainside and I
found not a bolt or nut or bell of a train.

I came to the bend where last we had seen it. I ran out on
the field where we'd sat and watched it go. Right then I developed what scientists called the gregarious instinct. I wanted
company and I wanted a lot of it. I didn't want to be on that
dusky mountain in the dark of the moon alone. I wanted to be
in a city with a million people around. I found myself in a panic.

I shouted at myself. I fired my Colt in the air. I turned right
around and fled back down that track, looking for a switch or
side-track or hole in the wall where that train could have ducked
after it left us up the hill. There wasn't any switch or side track.
There wasn't any hole in the wall. Banks jutted up on either
side of the track, solid rock. Then a cliff went up on one side,
and the chasm fell away on the other, dropping a quarter mile
to a flat stretch of sand, smooth and bare as glass with not a fly-

speck on it, far below. Then I was back in the canyon where Yole and Dr. Gobo had waited by the tracks near the *sablier* thicket.

Yole and the witch doctor weren't there by the track. They weren't waiting now. The only thing waiting there was a pair of shoes! I saw those shoes and I let out a howl that must have echoed to Cap Haitien. I pounced on those abandoned boots with that howl. Shoes! Yole's precious footgear!

You get it, don't you? I got it, believe you me! I tore up that bank, a shoe in each hand, and I thrashed through those *sablier* trees like a headless chicken. Yole and Gobo weren't there. I lunged out into a cane field. They weren't there, either.

"Yole!" I bellowed. "Gobo!"

No answer. No answer. And then there was an answer. It seemed to come from up on the morne, and then it seemed to come from down in the woods; and then I couldn't tell where it came from. But it throbbed through the jungle dark like the beat of a dark, sick heart, and it started me running without reason. *Boom!* came the faint sound. *Boom! Boom! Boom!* Then: *bum-bum-bum*, like quickened blood.

I fled down the mountain with the sound of that drum in my ears, and when I found my horse, the whole morne seemed to have taken up the echo. Day was coming in the east when the roofs of Cap Haitien appeared, and the drumming echoed off with fading darkness. I rode up to my bungalow with hot sunshine in my eyes, ice down my spine, and a pair of shoes in my hand.

CHAPTER V

I swear I've never been sicker thanI was the following two days. Tropical rain can give a man one of the highest temperatures recorded, and don't forget I'd been out in a first class tropical rainstorm. Then for forty-eight hours I scared the stuffing out of a Navy doctor sent up by the government station to take care of me, after my house man had dashed down into town saying there was a maniac in my bungalow who thought he had seen a pack of *zombies*.

I'll bet I scared that Navy medic into white hair. He said I kept hollering about dead trains run by dead engineers, engines fired with snakes, tracks that went over tottering trestles, corpses that waved from windows, oracles with goggles for eyes, and locomotives and men who vanished in thin air. He said I howled about a black express and a pair of empty shoes. He said I kept it up about the empty shoes until he had to shoot me full of morphine.

I must have given that doctor a woozy earful. The morning my fever broke he pointed at the pair of shoes under my bed, and told me I hadn't stopped yammering about them for twenty hours. He told me the fever had driven me mad as a hatter. He told me I had one devil of an imagination; packed up his kit and got into saddle and back to base as fast as he could go.

Well, I thought the whole affair had been a brainstorm. But there were Yole's empty boots, and there was the sound of drumming coming faintly down from the morne as the afternoon started to wane. When I heard those pulsing drum-beats and looked at Yole's shoes with no Yole around to wear them, I started in sweating all over again.

I went out on the veranda where Yole had stood not four

nights ago with the stamp of terror on his face. Once more the day had gone into mauve twilight, sunset was painting the sky with glory, dusk lay over Cap Haitien a kindly mask of beauty, and the tinted air was heavy with the scent of jungle flowers. Once again the morne above the town was a dreamy mount of shadows with clouds on its peak; and, again, from the heights where the clouds drifted, came that echoy throbbing. *Boom! Boom! Boom! Bum-bum-bum!* That beat.

This time it was I who stood in the twilight and twisted at the veranda rail while a growing serpent of fear tightened its coil around my brain. That Navy doc had told me I'd been hatter-mad with fever. But how about the night before I'd been down with the fever? Had I been mad then, and was I still insane? Had Yole and I really chased up that mountain railroad in a tempest; come to a chasm and a trestle on the rim of the world; encountered a *papaloi* witch doctor straight out of a nightmare; boarded a runaway train and jumped into a field and taken a short cut to find the train could totally disappear on its single track.

That ghastly express! Then nothing but empty track. Yole! Then nothing but his shoes!

I rushed back into the bungalow. Yes, there were the discarded boots. My pistol, then. As I remembered it I'd fired two shots from my pistol that night. One when I chased around a bend expecting to see Bombier waiting there with a rifle. The second I'd fired in that field bordering the jungle after I'd raced up the track and hadn't found the train. So I snatched up my automatic. Two bullets missing!

Someone was riding up the road from Cap Haitien. Hoofs clattering in the dusk. I rammed the accusing pistol into my belt. Went to the door, trying to screw my face into a look that would appear sane. A man dismounted at the gate; came hurrying to the veranda. A stranger. Trim in fresh white drill. Man with a long chin, mouth pressed thin, quick black eyes, flat cheeks unburned by tropic suns. As he stepped toward me I gained a fleeting impression that I'd seen him somewhere before. A U.S. official? I couldn't place him.

"You Mr. McCord?"

No, the voice was unfamiliar. He was new to Haiti. He yanked off his sun helmet and fanned perspiration.

"Mighty glad I've found you, McCord. Just came up from Port-au-Prince. Your consul here was there, and when I told him my story he said I'd find a Conrad Yole here, and if I didn't you'd be able to tell me where he was. Just now came from the Officers' Club. They said nobody'd seen Yole for the past two days."

His voice cracked with strain. "I've got to find Yole and find him in a hurry. If you help me it'll be worth your while, sir. I've been years locating him. Years!"

He produced a sheaf of legal documents. Shoved them in front of my eyes. I glimpsed the name, "Conrad Yole." A dim photograph. Description. "Born in Cap Haitien." More documents. My visitor stood there in the dusk, and somewhere way off in the twilight a drum was muttering, and my brains were going merry-go-round. Thoughts rode around in my head and I caught a brass ring.

I thought: "Sheriff's papers." And: "Yole—born Cap Haitien! Creole blood — " Yole always watching ships; hungry to get away. Telling nothing of his past. Scared of those voodoo drums.

"I've got to find him, sir!" the stranger insisted. "Will you help me?"

"I've a hunch!" I heard myself answering.

"Then you'll help? Damned good of you. Williams is my name. The consul will back me up. I'll make it worth your while if you lead me to Conrad Yole."

Well, I wanted to find Conrad Yole, too. Maybe you can understand why. This man with his sheriff's papers didn't want Yole half as much as I did. I never wanted to turn a man over to the law, but it was going to save something inside of me to see Yole again. And if my hunch was right he'd be a lot better off with this fellow than where he probably was.

So there I was riding up the morne again, automatic on

hip, in and out that maze of jungle, ravine and defile where bones grinned on posts and goats dangled down out of trees. The moon was queer that night. One of those moons that look like a decayed orange with one side squashed in. The sort of moon they paint in those terrible oval-shaped pictures made of mother-of-pearl. And the mountain that night was no more real than one of those gaudy scenes. The air static. Not a breath of wind. Just heavy, perfumed dark save where shafts of moonlight sneaked through foliage and lay in phosphorescent pools on the trail.

We rode in silence, Williams and I. I didn't talk, and the eerie atmosphere left him with nothing to say. Haiti on a moonlit night would get under any stranger's hide. Especially with the drums beginning.

Boom! Boom! Boom! Bum-bum-bum! The tuneless pounding throbbed through the dark, pulsating, uncanny, the beating heart of Haiti. Dark cliffs caught up the echo and tossed it from crag to crag. Canyon walls made resonant sounding-boards. The night vibrated. *Boom! Boom! Boom! Bum-bum-bum!* One drum started the thing. Thirty joined in. Now there must have been a hundred going with a beat that couldn't be stopped.

The velvet shadows, squashed-orange moon, funeral perfume of nocturnal flowers, moonlight in a tree where goats hung, a skull on a roadside post, and that maddening, loudening percussion —

My companion stopped once and exclaimed, "Good God!" After that he rode along with his hand on the butt of an automatic. I was glad to see his gun. If I knew anything about it, an American might need protection this night. I'd lived in Haiti a long time and never heard such hysterical drums before. The throbbing had my raw nerves jumping like an exposed tooth. Mad? I guess I was. A madman pushing his horse through a madhouse jungle night to save what was left of his mind.

Boom! Boom! Boom! As we climbed Morne Lune the tympanic darkness shook with the vibration. Farther up among the cliffs a mushroom of red haze flowered on the mountainside. The mushroom grew; glowing on the cheek of the night. It wasn't far under the summit of the morne. I spurred my mount and shouted at Williams to follow. That fire was the source of the drumming if I knew anything about it. As we neared the haze the drumming increased. By the time we were close enough to see the flames leaping in a grove of ceiba trees we could hear another sound. Voices chanting accompaniment to the drums. That undertone chanting made a weird witchery that poisoned the night. A bizarre choral timed to the thump of goatskin drumheads and the rattle of gourds. *Do, re, mi — do, re, mi — do, re mi* — The first three notes of the scale. A thousand voices chorusing the first three notes as if practicing some horrible vocal exercise. Over and over again. A nerve-racking repetition. *Boom! Boom! Boom! Do, re, mi! Bum-bum-bum! Do, re, mi!* First the drum; then the chant. Faster and faster. Exciting. Hysteric. Mind-blasting.

I didn't wonder that the muscles jutted in William's face. It was all I could do to quell an impulse to flee.

We'd found a path — mere suggestion of a trail through the brush — that seemed to lead toward the fire and the noise. Somewhere forward, I knew, was that infernal railroad curving up through the jungle. I couldn't think of that railroad. With that pulsating *Do, re, mi* mesmerizing your brain you couldn't think rationally of anything.

Now the fire had become a haystack of flame that outlined the huge ceiba trees in monster-like silhouettes. Sparks floated like giant fireflies among the mammoth, distorted black limbs. And the noise of drums and vocal chords towered like the smoke which rose and spread under the stars.

"Come on!" I heard a voice that wasn't mine urging Williams.

"This is it!" I wasn't quite sure what I referred to, but something told me a revelation lay ahead. Together we dismounted and went creeping through the underbrush toward the ceiba trees. I don't remember how long it took us to get there, but I recall very well what we saw when we arrived. That picture is etched on my brain with indelible inks. I'll never forget that glade on the brow of Morne Lune. That amphitheater where the jungle encircled an immense bonfire, black shadows went leaping, bellowing flame enameled red the dark.

Here the fire roar was smothered by the stunning din of drums massed before the door of the *houmfort* at glade's end. A hundred drums. All sizes and shapes. And a hundred drummers of all shapes and sizes were hammering like mad before the door of that little grass-thatched mystery house. Those cult zealots weren't all ex-slaves, either. I don't know where those cultists came from — they looked like worshipers assembled from Babylon and Gomorrah and other prehistoric Skid Rows. Why had they settled in Haiti?

Firelight gleamed on white faces, ebony faces, brown, gray-green, mottled, pink, yellow faces — a conglomorate that might've been recruited from the Tower of Babel. Sweat shone on pounding knuckles and swinging shinbone drumsticks. And if the drummers sweated, so did the dancers who cavorted, hopped and pranced around the leaping fire. Mouths wide, eyes rolling, heads bobbing, hands grabbing at the sky, that mob danced round the fire and squalled out *do, re, mi* — a voodoo-crazed St. Vitus fandango combining primitive mania, marathon jigging, early hard rock, the samba, bomba and shimmy with mass hysteria and Holy Roller frenzy.

What a camp meeting that was! Crouched on the amphitheater's edge, Williams and I had to clutch at roots to keep from rising straight up in the air on the swelling tumult.

And talk about weird costumes and devil masks! White teeth and wild eyes. Dervishes spinning and squalling had nothing on that Moon Mountain sect. Whew! Young women and crones, boys and men capered in carousal dance around the fire. Waving butcher knives, gourds, rattles. Tooting reed flutes. Banging tambourines. And there in the middle of the drummers before the grass hut the master of ceremonies! None other than Papa Gobo with his smoked goggles and plug hat, London doorman's coat, lace dress and all. High priest of the ceremony.

I got a nice jolt when I saw him presiding there, believe

you me. A shock right down to my heels. He had that sugary, exalted smile spread across his face, and his white-gloved hands were inspired as they'd never been before. You remember Al Jolson and Eddie Cantor and all those other black-face vaude-ville stars? Gobo was a cartoon copy of them all. Only he didn't sing. He bayed at the sky. *"Do, re, mi!"* leading the chorus with those pantomime hands, his expression angelic, his message something else again.

Three tall drums stood before him, and I knew what those drums were, all right. *Rada* drums from the most sacred of voodoo sanctuaries. Mama drum, papa drum, and baby drum. That's what they called them. Used only in the holiest of holy voodoo rites. Or unholiest of unholy, I should have said. For the minute I saw those drums I knew I was seeing something few non-Haitians had ever seen — a Petro ceremony. A blood ritual dating from the dawn of time.

Right then I wanted to get out of there, but I couldn't stir. I shot a glance at Williams, and by the looks of him he couldn't have twitched a finger. Like graveyard statues we knelt in those bushes, and the dance and drums and *do, re, mi* got louder and louder, faster and faster, till I felt I must foam at the mouth. And then the whole thing exploded in a perfect bedlam of sound, and the nightmare came to a climax.

The drummers tossed their sticks in the air, and backed away from the hut door. Williams' hand came shaking up from his belt, and he pointed a palsied finger past my nose. His shout was unnecessary. I saw Papa Gobo step aside from the door, and I saw the man who marched out of that grass house.

Yole! Yes, Conrad Yole. The merry-go-round of voodoo worshipers came to a dead stop and silence fell like a soundless bolt of thunder. And Conrad Yole came marching out of that little door bathed in red firelight. Yole in a plug hat and lace dress, with dark goggles on his eyes! A dead rooster in one hand and something I couldn't quite see in the other. Conrad Yole in the costume of an Oracle of the Dead! A barefoot, Haitian *papa-loi.* His face expressionless stone.

He walked out of that grass hut and straight into that frothing

mob of devotees and straight up to a pedestal near the fire. And when he mounted that pedestal you couldn't hear a sound. Even the fire seemed to go quiet. For one whole minute of hush Yole stood there motionless. Then Witch Doctor Gobo started the rune.

Do, re, mi. The mob took it up. The drums were like answering surf. *Boom! Boom! Boom!* The din resumed, louder and louder, faster and faster. Till Conrad Yole raised a fist high above his head; in that fist a gold knife. The gold knife paused. In a scurry the dancers closed in on the pedestal, bowls and cups suddenly in their hands.

"Stab!" screamed Papa Gobo. And Yole's golden blade started down.

And then Williams vaulted past me and hit that mob of fanatics with a roar. "Stop!" He sprang out of the bushes like a catapult, and his act smashed that ceremony like a mallet on a porcelain dish. I don't just remember what happened for the next ten seconds. I joined Williams and hit into a sea of madmen. I saw Williams go up on that pedestal; saw his gun whack Yole's chin; saw the pair of them come down. Then I saw nothing but teeth and lights and knives; and the next thing I knew I was legging it through the brush with Williams, Yole's limp body between us.

If you think those Haitian voodoo worshipers weren't infuriated, you don't know zealots. Crazy! It was no time for outsiders to monkey with the witchcraft soul, and those devils, robbed of their little suicide ritual, were wild as tigers with hydrophobia. Believe me, I worked my legs that night. So did Williams. It wasn't easy carrying Yole. Lord knows how we ever got out of there. I suppose those frenzied voodites tumbled over one another like clown cops, or we'd never have gotten away. As it was, one of those fiends did catch up with us.

We had crossed a field of bracken and come to the edge of a cliff, and I'll never forget that place if I live to be a thousand. The moon was bright as day, the scenery like a painting under a lamp. We pounded along the cliff rim, I say, and it dropped sheer to a ledge below, and then dropped off straight down for a quarter mile. On that ledge below ran the curve of railroad tracks. And far below the precipice stretched that expanse of clean, bare sand, yellow in the moonlight.

Can you visualize Williams and me running for dear life along that clifftop, dragging Yole in his masquerade costume between us? Then can you picture Papa Gobo coming after us, a gorilla from a zoo, his face contorted with rage, his butcher knife a silver horror in upraised hand?

"Shoot him!" Williams cried. I turned with a yell, and the automatic clicked in my fist. Jammed! As though by the evil eye!

The witch doctor sprang with a laugh. The machete lashed down. *Zaff!* It was close, that knife. I made a spine-wrenching dodge, and the blade came down like an ax on the barrel of my automatic. In a shower of livid sparks the gun went flying. I struck out blindly with a cry. I hit with everything I owned. I struck that demon with everything I had. Square in the middle of that saintly smile. Papa Gobo's head snapped back. Papa Gobo spun like a pinwheel. He twirled through the brush, and he spun right over the rim of that cliff.

I saw his body strike the edge of the ledge, the tracks below, give an outlandish bounce into space; and drop through moonlight, turning slowly. The plug hat came off halfway down and the lace skirt spread out like bat wings.

Down and down the creature fell through the moonlight. I saw him hit that expanse of yellow sand. I heard the far-off thump. That body landed on the sandy floor far below. And as I stared, the body disappeared. The sand closed over the witch doctor as though he were a dead cockroach fallen in a pan of custard. And Papa Gobo was gone!

A maddened mob was coming. Williams and I picked up Yole and fled. I don't know how we ever won the race to Cap Haitien. I guess we couldn't have if my legs hadn't acquired a sort of second childhood, and my brain come out of the fog. But my brain had started ticking again, because a lot of questions had been answered and I had time to remember the quickest way home.

I wasn't crazy. I thanked all the gods there are when I realized I was still sane. That missing express train! I could understand, now. It had stood up there on the morne on the far side of that infernal trestle; just where it had been left standing with its slain crew by the government troops way back there in the Eighties. Maybe it had been stopped there in that tunnel. At any rate it had been there on the track with the remains of those revolutionary soldiers of fortune turning to leather on the floors of the cars; with Ti Pierre, himself, hanging a dead arm out of the cab window; with the engine going to rust and snakes building nests in the tender behind the cab. There it had stood, waiting for the brakes to rot away, or a tempest to steepen the grade of the tracks, or an earthquake jolt to start it going.

Maybe there was pirate gold on that train. Maybe just a few coins. At any rate the natives had been superstitious about it, and left it alone, not daring to cross that trestle. But old Bombier had dared. I'd like to have seen him swing across that swaying bridge in the storm that hit us that night we chased him. I can see him teetering across that section where the ties were missing, balancing on a rail over half a mile of emptiness. I see him doing that in my dreams. Anyhow, he did get across and board that train.

How did the train get going? Maybe Bombier hauled on a brake-lever by accident. But a bit of an earthquake followed that storm, and I'm inclined to think that's what started the old iron horse out of her stall. Once started, every rust-eaten brake shoe let go, and she came down that roller-coaster track heaven bent for election. Must have been a steep, straight grade for a starter; then all she had to do was coast.

Bombier must have got a beautiful punch when he felt that engine running away. I can see him tugging on levers. I'll bet he wasn't happy. By the look on his dead face when the curve threw him out of his seat, I should say he had expired of sheer fright. It took me a long time to recognize that face. I never guessed it till we'd jumped off the train, and then things happened to make me forget such a trifling detail. That was Bombier in the cab, though. Literally scared to death. Heart attack, I'd wager.

Anyhow, his dandy old engine was running wild when it hit that stretch out of sight around the hill. The curve along the cliff edge where I'd smacked Papa Gobo must have done it. The train, too, kept on going right out into space, I supposed, and took a similar quarter-mile dive. Crashing through underbrush farther up the mountain, Yole and I hadn't heard Old 999 plop down into that soft bed of sand. We were shouting too loudly to hear anything. And while we waited for the train, the train was burrowing down into the goo to a grave where it could rest until eternity. Quicksand! The biggest lake of quicksand I'd ever imagined. That explained the train's disappearance.

Thanks to Papa Gobo, I could ride like the very devil and tote my share of Yole along with Williams down to the safety of the coast. We left that mob of voodoo worshipers to gnaw on bones of frustration in their jungle lair on the other side of Moon Mountain.

EPILOGUE

"Didn't I tell you?" The florid cotton buyer broke the silence in the wake of McCord's narrative. "Didn't I say blood would tell? If it's born in a man he'll revert to type in the tropics. Go native, like this fellow Yole. Part creole like he was, he couldn't resist those voodoo drums. That's what scared him when he heard them on moonlight nights calling him away from civilization. All it needed was that Afro witch doctor and his crazy cult whooping it up after that train disappeared. Almost led him to sacrifice himself to the voodoo gods on Morne Lune. He was born to it, right? The drums in his blood got him."

Tamping his briar pipe, McCord looked up. Away off in the night somewhere drums were thumping faintly and blue moonlight cast its spell on the roofs of Port-au-Prince below. A warm breath of oleander whispered on the breeze, and a shaft of moonbeams found our veranda and discovered on McCord's face a wry smile.

"There's magic in Hispaniola, all right," he said aiming his pipe-stem at the nocturnal landscape. "This Caribbean atmosphere and all. It can become pretty hypnotic. And, like that beautiful oleander bush out there, deadly poisonous. It certainly intoxicated Yole." He paused, gazing off. "But I didn't tell you the final pay-off of this affair. First, about Conrad Yole."

He broke off to light his pipe.

"What about Yole?" we chorused.

McCord blew out his match. "All right." He eyed a puff of dissolving smoke. "Williams and I lugged him pack-saddle down to my bungalow at Cap Haitien. Stripped off his jungle-wizard costume and put him to bed. The doctor I fetched thought he'd been drugged with something — they have all kinds of

weird herb concoctions in these mountains — but the medic
assured me Yole would come around. 'He'll pull through,' I
passed the word to Williams. 'Okay, Mr. Fed. What did you want
of him?'

"Williams stared at me. 'You think I'm a Federal agent?' I
spluttered, 'If you're not, you must be a U.S. marshal of some
kind. Those legal papers you want to serve him with. Aren't
they supoenas, or warrants?'

"Williams shook his head. 'Good heavens, man, didn't I
inform you? Those papers aren't warrants or supoenas. They're
legal, yes. But they're only to prove Yole's identity.' "

McCord blew an exclamation point of smoke. He watched
it dissolve. Then, "So. Here's the word on Yole. True, living
down here in the Caribbean he'd become unnerved by those
native drums. No question he was scared of a creole ancestry.
Afraid of going native, for a fact. Yole knew he'd been born in
the West Indies, which had troubled him. You see, being the
adopted son of a missionary, he'd never been sure just who his
real parents were. There are a lot of racial strains down here in
the islands, and the thought that he was part creole worried him
no end."

McCord gestured at the moonlight. "It's an eerie incandescence down here, you have to admit. Mix in a little rum and
some dance drums, and you can see how this lunar shine might
lead to lunacy. But Yole needn't have suspected his birthright.
Look. Remember I'd thought this man Williams looked vaguely
familiar when I first met him? Well, for months Williams had
been poking around the West Indies asking questions, exami-
ning local records, looking for a younger brother who'd been
kidnapped in the islands when he was a baby. He'd been snatched off his father's yacht. In Williams you could see the family
resemblance. And he'd finally traced Yole thanks to a native
who remembered the Quaker missionaries who'd adopted the
stolen infant. The Yoles weren't his true parents, no. He'd been
born with a totally different pedigree. He was christened Prescott
Williams."

Frowning, the cotton buyer asked, "What was his Williams ancestry?"

McCord smiled. "Old American family from Boston. Lowells, Cabots, Lodges — all that Back Bay stuff. Except his ancestors actually did come over on the Mayflower."

The cotton broker shrugged. "A blue-blood exception to prove my rule perhaps."

"He wasn't the only one," McCord said.

"What — ?"

"I think Papa Gobo was more of a surprise package."

We echoed, "Papa Gobo?"

"Listen." McCord aimed his pipe-stem at the Port-au-Prince waterfront. "After Williams identified Yole as his brother and they left Haiti for the States, the consul at Cap Haitien paid me a visit. Authorities wanted to know about Papa Gobo and his voodoo cult up there on Morne Lune. I didn't go into details — who'd believe that train story? — but I told about rescuing Yole from that murderous cult ceremony. And how old Gobo had plunged off that cliff into a bed of quicksand."

"What's that got to do with my point about someone touched with the tar-brush going native?" the cotton buyer demanded.

"Why, its just blunts your point again," McCord said. "The local authorities — the crack Garde de Haiti — sent a squad up there to clean out that voodo cult's vulture's nest. They arrested most of those crazy zealots and deported them. They'd have deported Pappy Gobo, too, if they'd caught him alive. Of course, when they found him he was dead."

"They found him? I thought you said he sank in a bed of quicksand."

McCord said, "The Haitian police spotted the place where he'd gone under, and they dug him out. No *zombie* ceremony could ever revive Gobo's corpse — every bone in his body was broken by that dive down the cliff. But the police did manage to record his fingerprints. Guess why? Well, down there in the muck the plunge had sandpapered Gobo's complexion to a cream color. It seemed he'd been going black-face with a minstrel-show mask of grease paint — they found a can of make-up in his grass temple — a regular Dixie mammy-song disguise.

"And who was Papa Gobo? A fraud wanted in three Southern Dixie states. Phoney spell-binder who once posed as a soul-saving, sawdust-trail tent-show evangelist. Wanted for swindling on church funds, misleading gullible people, and inducing converts to give their all to his cult. Also for the seduction of a schoolgirl in his Pied Piper flock. A peddler of sex and salvation.

"Dodging to Haiti to peddle witchcraft he'd learned in Louisiana, he'd found a ripe field for the plucking. But the point is Gobo was a white man. Name: Billy James Parker. From Oil Town, Oklahoma."

"But how," the cotton buyer asked, "could the Haitian police have found his body? If he plunged into a bed of quicksand that could bury that ghost train?"

McCord tapped his pipe into his palm. "I'm afraid you said the magic word," he advised his questioner. "Quicksand. The Haitian police spotted the tail of Pappy Billy James Gobo's priestly nightgown which had drifted to the surface. So it seemed the bed of quicksand wasn't very deep. In fact, it seemed it wasn't what we think of as quicksand at all. And for a further fact, nothing is."

We uttered an amalgam of exclamations. Ending with, "What do you mean?"

"Okay," McCord said. "After that police report, I consulted a scientist, a geologist working with a mining company in Haiti. 'Forget it, McCord,' he told me. 'There's no such thing as a great bed of quicksand up there in the Morne Lune area. How do I know? For one thing, because I've explored every valley in the region. For another, there's no such thing as quicksand, anywhere. Not if you mean a bottomless sink of loose wet or dry sand that supposedly can suck any man or animal inexorably into the depths, pulling the victim under the surface. Such a sand trap is bunk.'"

McCord gazed off at the velvet dark. "That's what the geolo-

gist said — bunk. He called quicksand an old wives' tale, one of
those folklore myths that persist in spite of modern research
and education. A deep-rooted fable without any scientific dem-
onstration or provable foundation. Of course, today you may
read of quicksand in literature, fiction, perhaps even news
stories. Come to think about it, though, where does it really exist?
Do you know of anyone who ever wandered into quicksand?
Ever see any warning signs that say 'Danger. Quicksand ahead?'
No, according to the geologist the stories about it are like those
press reports that begin, 'It is said,' or come from what's called
'a reliable source' — reports that are always anonymous with
nobody named who can be pinned down.

"The geologist told me quicksand tales were like that —
supposition or hocum. Typical was the rumor of quicksand
somewhere on the banks of the Kaw River in Kansas, nobody
could say just where. It appeared Boston Corbett, the soldier
who claimed he shot John Wilkes Booth, disappeared in that
part of Kansas some year after the Civil War. And folks declared the quicksand got him. But nobody saw him go under,
nobody witnessed that finale; no one really knows what became
of Corbett. The geologist asked me to ponder it. He thought
Corbett was probably murdered and the quicksand fable was a
cover story.

"Oh, he conceded Pappy Gobo sank in a soft bed of gooey
wet sand on the fringe of a dry lake. But the goo was silt washed
down from a mountain stream — a bed only about three feet
deep, with solid rock beneath. Bottomless quicksand, no.

"Don't think I didn't ponder." McCord gazed off. "I'm still
pondering. If there's no such thing as quicksand, what became
of that runaway train? Jumping off a cliff into a shallow bed of
muck, it would have sprawled like a half-buried junkyard down
there. What happened to those tons of iron? The police never
found a scrap of it — not a single nut or bolt — in that Morne
Lune gulch or anywhere else."

McCord shook his head. "Another thing. Without steam,
how did that whistle blow? A burst of some kind of gas released

by a breaking valve when the engine jolted into action? Gas, say, from rotted fungus, or a nest of dead snakes, or the decayed corpse of some gold-seeker who had crawled into the boiler, shut the lid, and couldn't get out? Something like that, maybe.

"But what could explain the train's vanishment? There was one far-fetched possibility. A mud-slide or landslide. An avalanche triggered by those earthquake tremors we felt up there on Morne Lune. Suppose the train jumped the track on that hairpin curve before the approach to Yole's shortcut? And the plunge into a ravine brought down an acre of mud or gravel that buried the wreck. Up there in that remote Haitian wilderness the grave of even a train might be hard to find in moony jungle. So that could've happened.

"Except I don't think so," McCord concluded.

"Then what did happen to that train?" we asked.

He lifted his shoulders, expressing bafflement. "Was it all an illusion? Mirage of some kind? Had Yole and I been drugged by Bombier when he fed us at his hut? Were the two of us hypnotized by Papa Gobo's tricky pantomime? I wondered. But I have to admit I had to wonder something else. Was that voodoo express an actual ghost train conjured by creole magic? A spectre that materialized and disappeared, evaporating like the echo of its whistle.

"Well, I saw that thing a long time ago. Haiti is not so primitive today. The people are better educated. Drive automobiles. Wear shoes. Or sandals, anyway. Like I do. Me. One hundred percent Yankee.

"But like them — for all my Anglo-Saxon background — aren't we brothers under the skin? — I can still hear that train-whistle. It wakes me up on full-moon nights. I'm left," McCord said, "with nothing but a line from Shakespear. 'There are more things in heaven and earth, Horatio, than you've ever dreamed.' You know the quote. I have to agree." McCord nodded at the night. "And a lot of those things are down here by the Caribees. Under that Haitian moon."

THE WONDERFUL LIPS OF THIBONG LINH

by Theodore Roscoe

THE WONDERFUL LIPS OF THIBONG LINH

"But I was once a deserter from the French Foreign Legion," said Old Thibaut Corday one night when we were discussing the iron-handed exactions of that famous army whose code is Honour, Valour and Discipline — especially Discipline. "You are surprised? But I was thirty years in the Legion, my friends, and it would be a rare Légionnaire who did not go over the wall at least once in thirty years. There are pictures on the walls of our barracks rooms that show what happens to Legion deserters when caught by hostile natives — but they do no good. There are the stone quarries at Oujda where apprehended absconders break rock in the chain gang for fourteen hours a day — it does no good, either. Also there is that terrible disciplinary corps called the Zephyrs, and for deserters in wartime there is always the firing squad, but sooner or later a Légionnaire will try it. *Bleu!*" the old Frenchman reproached himself for recklessness. "I took a chance with the firing squad. I deserted in wartime."

The tall American across the table lowered an un-gulped pony of cognac. "Gee — your post must've been pretty hard, to make you go on pump against odds like that."

"On the contrary, it was softest post of all the World War. Compared to some of the fronts I saw it was a flower garden."

"The officers, then," the American suggested. "You had a bunch of brutal officers?"

"Not so, *monsieur,* but some of the best I have known in the Legion." Praise from a Parisian who'd had to enlist as a Swiss.

"I know." It was the British consular agent, leaning out of shadow with a chuckle. "As the French say — *Cherchez la femme.* Am I right, Corday? You deserted the Foreign Legion because of a woman."

"You are right in one way," Old Thibaut Corday snapped, " and in another you are not. Let me tell you, it would have taken something more than a woman to make me jump the Legion at a time when the Germans were on us. And this woman was something more, too. She was a goddess, *messieurs.* The most wonderful goddess you ever heard of, and that includes Venus and Minerva and Aphrodite. Those lovely deities were unattractive alongside the one of whom I speak; for beguiling men she would have made that Greek siren, Circe, look like a Gascon fish-wife."

"She must have been beautiful," murmured the American.

The veteran soldier of fortune, whose bayonet-sharp eyes and cinnamon beard had come untarnished through a dozen wars, nodded emphatically. "Even though her eyes were crossed. Even though her nose was broken. Even though she had a finger missing and the nail gone from one toe. What? It was her lips, *messieurs.* They whispered in my ear to give me ideas like opium dreams. They drove me mad. They made me forget the War and desert the Foreign Legion. I have never told you about the wonderful lips of Thibong Linh? They told me the two greatest things in the world! But it is a strange chapter from my life, I assure you — perhaps the strangest chapter in the unwritten history of the Legion — certainly the strangest story of all the World War. You are not going to believe it unless you listen through to the end. You promise to listen through to the end?"

We promised.

Old Thibaut Corday dismissed Algeria beyond the café awning with a hand-wave. "It did not happen here in Africa. It happened in Asia. In Cambodia. Only in Cambodia could such a thing have happened — "

CHAPTER I

It is a tribute to modern civilization that the World War should have reached Cambodia, *messieurs*. One must pause to admire the marvels of transport and communication that our Western nations have developed. There is Cambodia tucked up in a corner of French Indo-China, a million miles from Paris and Berlin. Without transport and communication — and not being able to read the Christian newspapers — Indo-China would never have heard about the War. *Non*, her people would have stayed home peacefully smiling into lotus ponds and twining blossoms in their hair. Those dreamy Annamites and Tonkinese, they would never have heard of bayonets and machine guns and Christianity. They could not have gone to France and died heroic deaths in the mud. They would never have seen the Foreign Legion. Think what they would have missed! The War to end war in 1915.

Even so, the War did not do well in Cambodia. It was hard to make the natives understand why they should dress up in soldier suits and go to Europe to kill people. The recruiting sergeants tried to explain the glory of hand grenades, and the mission priests offered stirring prayers for patriotism, and those lazy IndoChines sat around dreaming. There was a lot of trouble about teaching them how to use bayonets, and so, early in the War, the Foreign Legion was sent out there to give them some private lessons. Imagine those stupid little people trying to resist civilization like that back in 1915!

Alors, we could teach the natives a little about war, but the country itself was impossible. One must have mud, rubbish, ambition for war. Fields to burn. Buildings to blow up. Bitter

145

desert or cold rain — those are things that inspire the proper martial spirit. It is easy to hate in a cold rain. And Cambodia is warm, tropical. Too sleepy for progress. Its towns were too old to blow up. Its fields too drowsy. I said it was like a flower bed.

You can't fight in a flower bed.

Do you know Saïgon, on the coast? The days there are scented with vanilla, the nights as soft as liquor and far-heard violins. The spell of the East is brewed in that city of parks and paper lanterns and toy pagodas surrounded by jungles of hibiscus, frangipani and tamarind trees. How could you haul seventy-five guns down a road where trumpet vines tangled in the cannon wheels and the native gunners kept forgetting what they were doing and would stop to eat an orange or pin a blossom behind an ear? There wre lily pools in a No Man's Land of pink and lavender, and you had to mount guard through long purple evenings lit with fireflies. Temple bells tinkled at dusk, and the café sold wine that tasted like rose leaves. It was not good for Légionnaires, that atmosphere. We yawned at drill and were late for parade. That softness was too much after campaigns in Flanders and Africa. Like drinking *crème de menthe* after a diet of gasoline. That country was no good for war. Not in those innocent days.

Our navies made the best of it, though, and there was some civilized fighting in the South China Sea. The German cruisers shelled some coastal villages, killing a lot of children and fisher folk. That would teach them to jump faster! It stirred up recruiting among the natives, and the U-boats taught them another lesson when they sailed for France. One transport after another was sunk when it left for Europe. At last there was some real civilization around there! Hoch the Kaiser, *non?*

One night I was summoned to headquarters at the marine barracks on Quai Francis Garnier. Consider my dismay at finding myself before the General Staff. After numerous questions and serious head-nods, I was told I would do. For what? Our Legion *commandant* took me into his office for a private talk.

He pulled the blinds and shut all the doors before it began. Then he told me because of my good record of only being drunk four times since the Legion came to IndoChine, great honor was to be conferred on me.

"Corday, it seems there is a war going on somewhere, and the Legion hasn't done a thing around here except to drink and drill these stupid yellow natives. But it is hard enough to make soldiers of these Cambodians without having the Boche drown them by the boat-load the minute they sail out of the Me-Kong. For the past six months every troop ship to leave Saïgon has been stopped by a tin fish." He banged the desk to show me how serious it was. "And that is where the Legion comes in!"

I suppose my face was blank. The *commandant* read my look.

"One would believe it is a matter for the French Navy," he agreed, "but as usual the Legion is called upon to do everything. The chief of staff thinks we should do something, since we are here to police this ridiculous colony. What is the War doing away off here in Asia, anyway?" He shrugged disgust; then glared. "Of course you know why all those troop ships are being sunk."

I said something about the U-boats being everywhere.

"The German spies are everywhere," he corrected tartly. "Espionage. Our ships leave port always under secret orders, and the Boche submarines find it out as if it had been in newspaper headlines. The German spies are thicker in Saïgon than the crazy ideas in the Kaiser's head. *Dieu!* we have shot dozens. Still they intercept our wireless, eavesdrop on our telephones, steal our code. Right now they are probably listening under the floor. That would be too bad," he grunted humorously as I jumped, "because I am giving you a message those Boche agents would love to get. It carries special instructions to our northern naval base at Hanoi, and you are to detour via Cambodia on foot and take it there on a *mission extraordinaire* by a deceptive, roundabout route."

So that was what my good record had let me in for! I was to carry a secret message five hundred miles to the north, follow the jungle trails on foot, go alone, and probably be chased by

German spies all the way. I protested I knew nothing about dispatch bearing and less about Cambodia. Exactly why they were sending me! German agents would never suspect a common Légionnaire, and maps would tell me all of Cambodia I wanted to know. Two Tonkinese guides would meet me at Battambang. *Dieu!* Before I could think of an out, I was handed the secret paper, given money, maps, a password, and told to start as soon as I could pack a havresack.

"You have thirty days — a month — to reach Hanoi. Take your time or hurry, use your own discretion. Foes may try to stop you; they may even kill you," I was told, "but if you talk to nobody — listen to nobody — you will probably be all right. Remember the winning of the War may depend on your delivering that paper. Remember the great trust our army has put on you. The honour of France and the Foreign Legion is in your hands. Get there!"

Sacred Saint Sulpice! that officer shook hands in a way that said "good-bye" too decidedly for comfort, and the next minute I was out in the night with all the responsibility of the War on my shoulders. Talk about your Message to Garcia! In that Asian wilderness Hanoi seemed as far away as the moon, and my life wasn't worth a *piastre* with that document in the lining of my coat, and as I walked up Quai Francis Garnier under the stars I could see a German spy peering out from behind every hibiscus blossom. I hummed the *Marseillaise* off key for courage, and decided I would start for Hanoi that very night. I would talk to nobody and listen to nobody. France, the Legion depended on me. I was scared and proud and determined not to fail. You would hardly have thought it the time for one so burdened to fall in love.

But I walked into a side street off Rue Catinat to have a drink before I started on that perilous journey, and that is what happened, *messieurs. I repeat, only in the East could it have happened. A fist shot out of a black doorway and knocked me down. I looked up, and fell in love! I fell in love for life.*

I fell in love that instant.

CHAPTER II

Not that I knew I was in love then! All I knew was that a fist had hit me in the eye, and when I glared up from the paving I saw a gang of yellow ruffians fighting around a woman. A paper lantern hung in a window across the alley, and its frail light showed me about ten of those dogs — greasy Me-Kong boatmen, by the looks — scuffling fiercely in that doorway. One of the curs had swiped me by accident, and I would have sprung up in fury, but I had to stop a second and grab my breath. I grabbed a mighty big breath, I can tell you! The woman in that doorway was in a bad way. It did not need the terror on her face to tell me that. She was backed against a plaster wall, a tiny silk-wrapped figured clutched against her bosom, and with her free hand she was lashing a bamboo switch at that swirl of evil faces.

But it was not that which made me fill my lungs. *Non!* It was her beauty. Never had I seen a woman like her. Never! Those river rats clawing at her were natives, and she, herself, was Asian — I knew that at a glance — but her beauty was something beyond complexion, race or country. Even in terror she was beautiful. The taut curve of her throat, the glow of her eyes, the exotic magnificence of her courage (I thought of a flower doing battle with hornets) as she lashed at her assailants. Many times afterwards I wondered about her, *messieurs.* When I saw her in calm. Her eyes like moonlight in the fragile oval of her face; her gentle, shapely hands; her feet in tiny sandals; her skin of palest sulphur in a sheer ice-blue sarong — where was she from? She was not Annamite, Lao or Tonkinese. She was not any of those races of Cambodia or the China Coast. Her beauty was not of this world. Do you know what she made me think of when

150

first I saw her, fighting to protect that small bundle in her arm?
The Madonna — *La Giaconda.* The Madonna as she might have
looked, fighting to keep her child from Evil.

"Devils!" I shouted, plunging into the fray. "Attack a woman
with a child in her arms — !" *Sacré!* the sight of those brutes
striking at her made me blind with rage. She had been fighting
magnificently, uttering no sound, and that doorway battle had
been silent as a scuffle of cats. But she gave a low cry of thank-
fulness as I reached her side, and that cry was enough to make
me fight like a wildman. I had to fight, too. Those curs were on
me like wolves, and only then did I remember I had gone to the
Marine Barracks unarmed. *Bleu!* I was suddenly in the vortex
of a cyclone of knives, in the devil of a brawl. Before I had time
to howl for the police I was crowded into a sort of hallway off
the alley, a door was slammed, and I was battling tooth and nail
in the pich dark.

"Légionnaires! Aidez-moi! Au secours!"

My shouts were blotted by close walls and a smell of dank
plaster. Knives came from all directions, and I could hear
slippered feet running down a stairway I couldn't see, more rats
joining the riot. Twice I went down under the pack, and I had
thought the woman was finished when suddenly her hand was
on my wrist, her low voice at my ear.

"Quick! Quick! This way! There is a passage here. Hurry,
or they will kill us!"

To this day I do not know how we got into that passage. It
seems to me she pulled me up by the arm, and then, as if we had
gone through the wall by some manner of magic, we were running in a place like a tunnel, an underground corridor that bent
and burrowed through the blackness as rabbit's hole — all the
ferrets in the world coming after us. I would like to know about
the tunnel under Saïgon. I would bet it was dug in a day before
Marco Polo. A good many days before. We may pave the streets
of Asia with concrete ten feet thick, but underneath she remains
the same. She keeps the same secret panels and hidden passages

under her surface as she keeps in her mind. We ran a long time in that tunnel under there. We ran out of the present and back down the ages a thousand years, as you will see. We ran right out of reality.

But it was real enough under there with fifty assassins at my heels, and I ran like mad to keep up with the woman. She would touch my hand to lead me around a turn, and sometimes I followed her scent. Her fluttering sarong left a perfume in its wake that was like the quick breath of a suddenly opened porcelain jar, a perfume as strange as a Chinese Garden, as delicate as a moonflower, as tenuous and unknown as some secret from Thibet. Even while running for my life it intoxicated me; seemed to lighten my heels. It was strange in that pitch-black tunnel. It made me feel as if I was running after a rainbow.

But a couple of times I banged my head into unseen corners, fell down on loose stones, tore shreds from my elbows on invisible walls. Once when I took a tumble those ferrets behind almost caught me. It was no time to suddenly remember the paper hidden in my tunic, the mission entrusted me by France. Thousand thunders! I couldn't die in that rat hole before I had even started. Imagine that! To be butchered by a huggermugger gang of Cambodian river rats, and not even give the agents from Berlin a chance! I cursed the luck that had put a woman on my hands, and at the same time I knew I could not let the dogs behind us kill her. Humanity came first. The War Department would not see it that way, but departments are never human, only the people in them are. Any Frenchman would have tried to help that woman. I told myself I would get her out of there.

As a matter of fact, she got me out of there. I suppose we ran two miles — I have no idea — but with the suddenness in which she pulled me into that passage, she pulled me out of it. A quick side-turn. A breath-taking door. More magic, and we were out in the night, running in one of those lotus-pooled jungles that make of Indo-China a warm botanical garden. Through the maze of orchid-hung palms and tamarinds the woman's silk-clad body slipped and flashed like a moon-seen fish. She stopped

abruptly in a glade bowered with ferns; stood finger to lips, listening. Then she sank down on a knoll, hugging her tiny, wrapped-up burden.

"We are safe for a while, I think." Her voice was husky, speaking French in a quaintly accented whisper. "They have taken the wrong turning. It will be some time before they discover our track."

She settled back on an elbow. "Come. We must regain our breath." She carried over her shoulder a beaded reticule. From it she now extracted what looked like a perfume bottle. It was not perfumery. She took a sip, then held it toward me. "Here. This elixir will revive you."

Who was I to decline a drink? Elixir, she called it. Oof! Whatever that ambrosia was, it hit me behind the belt like the hoof of an army mule. I know it was not absinthe. And it was not Pol Roget. It sank me into a crouch — *voila!* — with my head in a momentary daze. When my vision cleared, I felt much better. That is, I floated to a reclining position beside her.

She took from her reticule a cheroot. Holding it delicately in her teeth, she lit it with a wax Chinese match — her reticule seemed to be a veritable commissary of goods — and after taking a gentle puff, handed it to me. "You would like a good cigar, *mon brave?* Of course." She smiled. "All military men like good cigars."

Military men! That is what got me. How could a lowly dog of a footsoldier refuse? So I saw no harm in lingering long enough for a few puffs of that cheroot. Resting on an elbow beside her, I puffed. Figure that, if you can! That scene! You would have thought it was peacetime and we were somewhere up the Seine River, posing in one of those picnic paintings by Renoir.

If it seems unsoldierly, looking back, I remind myself that we Foreign Légionnaires seldom could save up the price of a cigar. And never such a cheroot as that one. The leaf smelled of the finest tobacco. Three puffs — that and the drink — had me as relaxed as warm India rubber. I saw that woman's face through the halo of a smoke ring — a portrait right out of the Louvre —

and I could not get my rubber legs to stand me on my feet and march out of there. I should have been watching the jungle, but I could not get my eyes off that delicious female.

I have an idea this knightly romance might have warmed up to something not so knightly at that point, if she had not reminded me of the burden she so bravely bore.

She parted a fold in the bundle in her arms; peeped down at a face I couldn't see; then her eyes looked up into mine with a thanks that rewarded me for my rescue-act a million times. Dizzy, I stared at her. It was time for me to clear out of that; but the strange circumstances of our exit from Saïgon to this moon-lit bower, the revealed beauty of that woman, held me as before a mystery. In that glade she was lovelier than ever. An oval face framed in a casque of jet hair. Complexion of faintest lemon tint, and that electric-blue sarong which fitted her like her skin. Sculptors from the time of Athens had been trying to find such a figure, and painters trying to find such eyes. When I looked into their deep clarity I felt as if I were drowning. *Oui*, I had to pull myself up with a shock. Somehow I got to my feet.

"Where are we?" I panted. "We must return at once to Saïgon."

She pointed over my shoulder, and by parting some ferns I could look across a night-blue valley to a scroll of lights that seemed miles beyond the jungle's fringe. The sight of those city lights put me in a sweat to get back there. *Mon Dieu!* I was supposed to be carrying a military message to Hanoi. I motioned the woman to come, but she shook her head.

"They would kill me in the city. I am safer here."

"Who are they?" I snarled. "And what would they kill you for?"

"They are bad men," she whispered. "Very bad men. They would kill me for this." She patted the little bundle cradled in her arms, and once more fear was on her face. "I dare not go back to Saïgon."

"But you must!" I told her desperately. "I will take you to the Legion barracks, put you under the protection of the army.

The French police will protect you from those kidnappers. I have got to go, and you must come with me."

Again she shook her head. "It was brave of you to help me. You have saved my life, and I would not imperil yours. Go! I will stay here."

"But I can't leave you here in the jungle," I cried. Her face was pale in determined resignation, and sweat streamed on my forehead at this emergency. "I can't leave a woman and a child — !"

Do you know what she said then? I would wager a thousand francs you cannot guess, but it would not be a fair bet, *messieurs*. I had started for her with outstretched hand to make her come, and what she said, then, rooted me to the ground like a banyan. Embracing that little silk-wrapped bundle, she drew back from my reach.

"It is not a child," she whispered. "It is a goddess! I am the Priestess Thera, and the goddess is in my care. It is the goddess, Thibong Linh —!"

Well, that was something to choke on, was it not? I give you my word, I swallowed six times before I could get a spoonful of air. If that woman had told me she was Mother France with the cherished L'Aiglon against her bosom, I would not have been more unraveled. But because I did not know about the goddess, Thibong Linh, she informed me.

Alors, I learned a lot about her — not as much as I was going to, but enough to be astounded. Even a Légionnaire could not be long around Cambodia without hearing some of its religious legends; like most Asian countries, Cambodia is soaked in religions. Confucious got around there, and Buddha with Lao-Tse at his heels, long before the Bible. Those religions mixed and exchanged ideas, the same as Christianity borrowed its monks from Mithraism and some of its ceremonies from Egypt; and lost somewhere in the mix-up in Cambodia was Thibong Linh. You can see how lost she was when I tell you she was the Goddess of Truth. She did not have any more followers in Cambodia than she would have had in Paris or New York. She would not have been followed at all if something else hadn't been lost with her. But her immortal image was supposed to hold the secret of a vast treasure, a tremendous fortune that some ancient devotees had buried in her honor. One legend had it that the devotee had inscribed the location of the treasure on one particular image. That brought the goddess some followers! *Oui,* that started the adventurers hunting Thibong Linh from one end of Asia to the other.

But Truth proved as hard to find in Asia as in Europe or America, its treasures as deeply buried. The trouble was to find the right image. The East is as full of old images as a dog of fleas, and a lot of them look alike. You can imagine it gave me a twist when that woman said she had Thibong Linh in her arms. The real, the true Goddess of Truth.

"You are the priestess, Thera?" I burbled. "And that is the goddess, Thibong Linh — ?"

"The goddess was entrusted to my care by the monks of the Temple of the Moon at Angkor Wat," she whispered. "Those Buddhist renegades were trying to steal her, and I was told to bring her to Saïgon for safekeeping."

The Temple of the Moon. Angkor Wat. Those whispered names had an exotic something that went through my head like the wafts of rare perfume released from the woman's delicate sarong. That wasn't all that went through my head, either. All at once that beautiful priestess was telling me the story of Thibong Linh, the story of the Goddess of Truth, a story no easier to believe than some of our Old Testament tales, but just as virtuous and wonderful.

It had come down through the East-tarnished ages, that parable of Thibong Linh, the Cambodian Queen who once told lies. No other queen as beautiful ever sat in the palace at Pnompenh; princes fainted, overcome when they looked at her; her face was lovely as a lotus, and most beautiful of all were her lips, soft and curvy as rose petals kissed with dew. And that was a pity, for her mouth was false, a fount of black prevarication.

Always she lied. Ask her the weather on a golden day and she would say it rained. Ask her who broke the jade pitcher at the bath and she would blame someone else. Never, never, never did she tell the truth. The habit of lying grew on her, and it was dangerous, for people believed her because of the innocent look of her lips. Her falsehoods got the country into an epidemic of troubles, courtiers were unjustly accused, marriages broke up, and at last a perjury to a neighboring king brought on a war in which thousands were slain. The sacred Buddha heard of that, and decided it was time to take a hand. In the form of a white dove he appeared before Thibong Linh and told her that henceforth every time she spoke an untruth her body would shrink an inch. Thibong Linh told Buddha she would never tell another lie, and straightway her body shrank an inch. She denied that she had shrunk at all, and down she went another inch. That scared her.

But try as she would, she could not stop lying. The habit was too fixed on her, and in three weeks she had dwindled to a midget, a queen hardly sixteen inches tall. She realized then that Buddha wasn't fooling, and if she kept on fibbing she would be reduced to nothing. At that point the little queen determined she would always give honest answers.

Then the politicans stepped in to make it hard for her. She was much too honest for any court, and they wanted to get rid of her. The wicked courtiers tried to force her into lies, asking all manner of tricky and embarrassing questions. Time after time she told the truth and sent them off in consternation. Finally they put their heads together, and the cunning court chamberlain said he knew how to shrink the queen to the size of a pin. "We will finish her now," he exulted. "I have a question no woman in the world will answer truthfully." Before a great gathering in the palace he faced the queen. He asked her her age!

The little queen told him how old she was, and when she gave her age truthfully, the listening Buddha was so pleased he made her a goddess! "From now on," Buddha told her, "your lips will always speak the truth. All knowledge is yours, and to any question asked of you, you will give an honest answer."

That was the story of Thibong Linh, the parable told me by that beautiful priestess there in that jungle. But I wish you could have heard it as she told it. Her voice a low, earnest murmur. Her eyes cast down worshipfully on the bundle in her arms. Moonlight on her face. If you had heard it as she told it, you would understand why I forgot those murderous coolies who had been chasing us, why I forgot the dangerous mission I was on, why I stood there like a child listening to a lullaby. And like all good story-tellers, she climaxed her fairy tale with a piece of drama I will never forget. By Saint Anthony's Fire! if I outlived the millennium I would never forget it.

"There is only one true Goddess of Truth," the beautiful priestess concluded softly. "When Thibong Linh died, Buddha decreed that her body should never go to dust, and he gave her to the monks of the Temple of the Moon. For twenty-four hundred years Thibong Linh has remained in what Westerners might call a state of suspended animation. Truth is eternal! She is not alive today; neither is she dead. Look! You would like to see the goddess — ?"

As she pulled the silk wrappings from the little thing in her arms, I suppose I swallowed a gurgle of dismay. You know how it is with Oriental legends. At the most, I had expected something remarkable in solid gold; at the least some sort of ancient, sacred mummy, some holy relic worth risking your life for. What the woman held up for my inspection was hardly a good carving, a thing of wood so old the grain had cracked and the paint had blurred and peeled — the sort of old image you could buy for a dollar in a Singapore curio shop. Except for the almod eyes and the Buddhistic lips in the cracked face, it resembled the *santas* I had seen in old Portuguese and Spanish shrines. There was no valuable inscription on it, either.

"Why, it's just a worthless shrine-piece," I cried. "Nothing more than an old wooden doll."

A look of reproach crossed that woman's moonlit face, and, hugging the image to her bosom, she recoiled as if from a blasphemy. "You do not know what you are saying, Monsieur Légionnaire! It is Thibong Linh, Goddess of Truth, Mistress of all the Verities. She sees all, knows all — "

I stared.

"And so does that cinema news reel which is trademarked with a rooster," I snapped, infuriated that I had risked my life and the secret plans of France to rescue a woman's wooden toy. "You can take your image and — "

"She answers all!" the woman continued, ignoring my outburst. "Any question you wish to ask of her, Thibong Linh will answer truthfully. It was so decreed by Buddha, and it is written that Thibong Linh will answer two questions of her between sundown and midnight — any two, but only two — and the truth will be given to the questioner. Do you understand now why those men would kill me to get her?" The woman's eyes were narcotic, shining up into mine. "It was she who told me of the tunnel which let us escape from that house tonight. One question she has answered; tonight she will answer one more. Is there nothing you would like to ask, Monsieur Légionnaire? Hold her lips to your ear and listen closely. Ask, and her lips will speak — !"

Well, that was the dramatic climax I have tried to prepare you for. I took that cracked wooden image from the woman's outstretched hands and held its silly face to my ear. Don't ask me why I did it. The soft voice of that lovely priestess was one reason, and the jungle-scented moonlight was another. I was mad at myself for doing it, too. That a Frenchman from the country of Voltaire, that a soldier of the Foreign Legion should be acting out such a farce!

"What are the two greatest things in the world?" I snapped. My eyes were on that woman sitting a few feet away on the knoll, and I felt like forty fools — asking a question of a painted piece of wood. "If you are really the famous Thibong Linh, answer that one. What are the two greatest things in the world?"

"Love and peace," answered a tiny voice at my ear. "Love and peace."

Messieurs, I dropped that image as if it were hot. *Bleu!* It was not just the voice in perfect French. The lips against my ear — the wooden lips had moved! And at that paralyzing moment a knife came sailing from the tamarind thicket behind me and buried itself in a tapang at my elbow!

CHAPTER III

And now from your expressions, *messieurs,* I see you have forgotten your promise to listen through to the end before disbelieving, and you think old Thibaut Corday is crazy. I do not blame you, *messieurs.* Turn me into a pepper mill, but I thought old Thibaut Corday was crazy, myself! I thought a little belt had slipped off the flywheel in my brain when I heard that voice from the image and felt its painted wooden lips moving against my ear. The dagger that had missed my shoulder-blades and twanged into a tapang tree did not bother me half so much as that image miracle. That scared me a lot more than the knife. I thought I was as mad as De Maupassant when he heard conversation in an empty room.

The woman screamed and caught up the image from where I had dropped it in the ferns.

"Run! Run! It is the brigands come to take the goddess! They would cut us to pieces for Thibong Linh! Follow me!"

She was flashing off through the undergrowth again, carrying the image as if it were a baby. I followed her. There was no hallucination about that knife hilt-deep in the tree, and the howling pack coming after us moved too fast for any doubting. All night I raced after that woman and that image through the jungle. And only when the sun burned a scarlet hole through the misty orchid veils in the east did the sounds of murder stop curdling the silence behind us. But the woman didn't stop going. Soundlessly she glided on and on through that flowery jungle welter, scarcely pausing to draw a breath. I was tired enough to fall on my nose as I stumbled after her.

With tropic daylight slashing my face and the reality of noon around me, I was sure that Thibong Linh business had been a

162

dream. It had to be a dream! That image in my hands had been nothing but a piece of carved wood, an old tarnished piece of carved wood, chipped and battered, the paint pastel with age, the gilt worn dim. Shrine-piece or not, a wooden image can't talk, and I knew I must have imagined that tiny voice.

But at the same time I knew I had not imagined those lips whispering against my ear. I had felt their movement with my skin — like the lips of a child pressed close to tell a secret — and the lobe of one's ear does not have that much imagination. Maybe you can understand why I threw all my senses to the winds and ran after the woman who had that marvellous image in her possession.

At noon we halted by a mossy-banked pool in a forest of palms and kaladangs, and for the first time since midnight the woman spoke, saying we ought to eat something and rest. Eat something? In the surrounding bowers of warm green the fruits and legumes hung like globes on Christmas trees, plump durians, wild oranges, pomegranates, crimson mangosteens. The very air had a flavor as delightful as custard; had the woman told me she had brought me to the garden of the gods I could not have disbelieved her. I was starving for one of those juicy jungle fruits, but the uproar in my mind was far greater than my appetite.

"Let me see it," I panted. "Let me see it in the daylight. Now!"

She smiled softly, putting the silk-wrapped object in my grabbing hands. *Non*, she made no protest as I tore loose the veilings and glared at the little image in my shaking fingers. In the daylight it looked more mutely wooden, more crudely carved than in the moonlight before. The nose was chipped, one finger broken from the folded hands. dented, weather-beaten, it looked as worthless as the figurehead of a Chinese junk. The mouth was all cracked.

"But the lips moved," I panted. "I felt them move last night against my ear."

"She was speaking to you, Monsieur Légionnaire. Thibong Linh was answering your question."

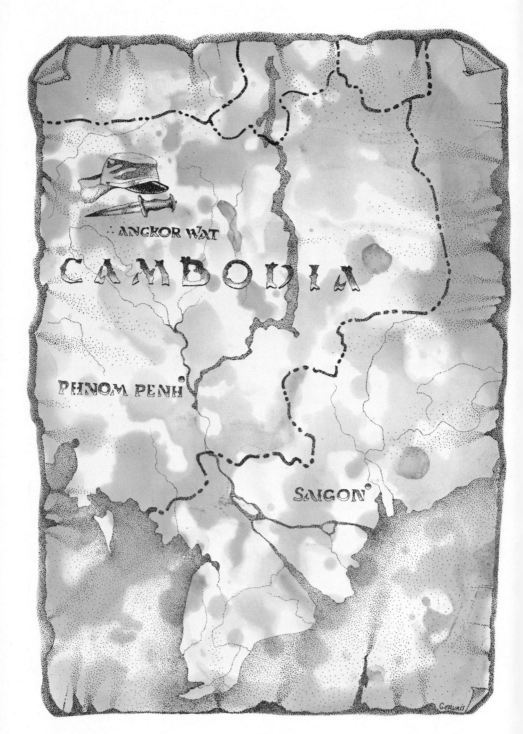

"If this image can really talk," and even to myself my whisper sounded mad, "it is just about the most valuable thing in the world!"

Taking the miraculous figure from me reverently, the woman shook her head. "She has revealed to you the two greatest things in the world, Monsieur Légionnaire. But you are right as to her priceless value. Imagine what the world would do to possess her. Imagine what men would do to own Thibong Linh who gives the truthful answer to all questions, who knows the secret of all life, the key to all worldly treasure — "

"I have a question I want to ask her!" I blurted. "Where — ?"

The woman was quicker than my outcry, putting two fingers against my greedy lips, two cool fingers that reproached my feverish grabbing and soothed the tumult of excitement and unbelief in my brain. "Not now, my good friend. You forget the sacred Word. Only between sundown and midnight will the lips of Thibong Linh answer questions — any two, but only two. And now we must rest . . . we must rest . . . " Again she offered that elixir.

It is hard to believe it, *messieurs*, but I sank down on that mossy bank like someone sleepy on a bed of cushions. My thoughts were whirling like a gramophone disk, but the warm custard scents of that Cambodian jungle, the lush green shade, the fatigue of an all-night relay race had induced in my body an impossible languor. Or perhaps it was the woman's soothing voice as she brought me a lapfull of food begged from a nearby farm. Or the calm strange beauty of her as she ate beside me on that green velvet bank, the fern-cooled sunlight on her face, goddess cradled in her arms, her reflection mirrored in the pool as a turquoise water maiden smiling from the placid depths.

"You like a cigar?"

Have you ever seen a doll smoke cigars? So Priestess Thera was herself a doll, *c'est ça*. She drew from her reticule that packet of savory cheroots. Again she offered me one — a gift no military man could refuse — then lit one herself. I had seen other native women smoking, of course, but never as delicately, as gracefully as my companion.

As for me, two puffs and I again relaxed in a rainbow-tinted mist. Those cigars of hers were different. None of your cheap bistro brands, your run-of-mill Turkish or Egyptian plug. This was the sort of perfecto leaf Omar Khayam must have smoked in his sacred hubble-bubble after his jug and loaf of bread.

But again I wondered if this luxury was robbing me of my mind. Do you know what the Priestess Thera did? She blew a slow, cool trickle of smoke through pouted lips. Then, smiling sleepily, she put her cigar to the lips of that little wooden doll. And — I swear this by my sainted grandmother! — that doll pulled a long whiff, and expelled a slow, cool exhale of cigar smoke. Exactly as had the priestess. If those cheroots were exhilirating, that was nothing to the jolt dealt me by that toy smoker.

Later on, evenings of cigar smoking became order-of-the-day routine. We would have our vagabond repast. Then the after-dinner cheroots. Talk about blowing smoke-rings! Priestess Thera blew rings around me those nights. And that doll, Thibong Linh, blew them around both of us. I do not expect you to believe such a tale, but you will see. The priestess smoked, the doll smoked, and so did I. Then Priestess Thera would hand me the doll, and I would ask it my village-idiot questions.

All of this stemmed from my second night under the moon with that lady. We were in the Garden of Eden. She fed me apples.

Do you wonder I smoked there beside her? That for the second time in twenty-four hours I forgot the alley fight, the rat pack coming after us, the desperate departure from Saïgon? *Eh, bien,* my mud-spattered uniform reminded me I was a Légionnaire, and that reminded me of my important dispatch to Hanoi, but the urgency did not seem so urgent somehow, and I told myself I had thirty days. And what was that compared to this woman and her marvellous possession? There was one more question I wanted to ask that Goddess of Truth!

The last thing I remember before drifting off to sleep was the fragrance of the woman's curve-moulded sarong. May I become a Gascon, then, if I didn't wake with twilight on my eyelids, the woman bending over me, her hand gently shaking my arm!

"Légionnaire! Légionnaire! Our enemies will be catching up with us, for they always travel at night. It is sundown, now! It is time to go!"

"Sundown!" I sprang to my feet. "And will the goddess answer questions now?"

"Any two, and only two! But we must hurry — hurry — !"

She handed me the wooden image and walked down to kneel on the mossy bank, drinking then from the clear pool. Ah, she was beautiful as she knelt in the mauve dusk, drinking. I had no mind for beauty, though. I can tell you, I hurried. Holding the head of the image to my ear as she had instructed me the night before, I put the question I had been choking to ask, in the rapid-fire tones of a lawyer in a court room.

"Where is the treasure that the fortune-hunters say was buried in your honor?"

Naturally, I knew the image would not answer. I knew it had all been a mental stunt. The dark-eyed woman had mesmerized me, and now she could not mesmerize me with her face bent over, drinking from the pool.

"The treasure of Thibong Linh is buried in the Vault of the Stored Moonbeams at Lu-ong Kuampur."

I did not drop the little image that time! Name of a Name! When I heard that minikin voice at my ear, felt the movement of those hand-carved wooden lips come alive, I was too excited to let go.

"How does one get there?" I asked in a voice that I had to extract from my liver. "How does one reach Lu-ong Kuampur to find the treasure vault?"

Again the occult pronouncement in perfect French. Again the whispery, baby-kiss movement of the image's lips. "Find the writing of Buddha on the wall of the Dragon Shrine in Angkor Wat. The writing will tell you how to reach Lu-ong Kuampur and the treasure of Thibong Linh — "

If you who are listening want to call me a liar and go home, I will not hold you to your promise in spite of my ability to keep mine. You remain? Too kind, *messieurs.* Then it will not be hard for you to believe how I went with that beautiful priestess to Angkor Wat.

With the spell of a miracle on my face, I went — all the laws of life and nature, the rules of existence which had held me to my obedient lock-step with the herd, turned to water on the brain. A wooden image had spoken in my ear; told me how to find a treasure. If an antique carving had moved its lips against your ear, revealing the hiding place of a million dollars, you would have gone with that woman to Angkor Wat, too!

And from there we went to Battambang, Stung Treng, Kompong Thom, and Pnompenh. Even the names of those places in Cambodia are like dreams, and our pilgrimage, going from Angkor Wat to those towns, was like a child's bedtime trip to the capitals of Never-Never Land.

Thibong Linh's treasure was not in the Dragon Shrine at Angkor Wat, you understand. We went there to read the writing of Buddha on the wall of that ancient ruin, and when we found the writing on the wall of that archaic cloister neither myself nor the woman could read it. I believe Buddha wrote that inscription, too. It looked like his handwriting. Angkor Wat was not built the day before yesterday. Archaeologists for three generations have been trying to solve the hieroglyphic mysteries of that venerable cluster of stone temples in the heart of the Cambodian jungle, a construction job finished in the dawn of Asia. Only there was someone in our party a whole lot smarter than an archaeologist. What do you think we did?

Why, we sat down to wait for sunset, and then I held the Goddess of Truth against my ear and asked her please could she translate the letters scratched in the ancient plaster? Yes, she could. Buddha had written: *Burn a rice paper before the Sacred Elephant at Battambang, and the next step toward the door of Thibong Linh's treasure vault shall be revealed to you!* And what, please, was the nearest way to Battambang? *Take the footpath through the swamp land southward, bewaring of the water buffalo!*

From there on it went like that. We burned a rice paper

before the Sacred Elephant at Battambang, and then we waited
for Thibong Linh to read the ashes — which told us to go to
Stung Treng, two hundred miles east as the crow flies. At Stung
Treng it was tea leaves. Tea leaves which the wooden image
read for me, directing me to a certain ancient monastery in the
jungle beyond Kompong Thom. We were out to find Thibong
Linh's treasure vault at Lu-ong Kuampur, you comprehend,
and neither the woman nor I knew where that place was, and
those were the steps we had to take to get there. One night it occurred to me to ask the image if there was not a more direct
route instead of — what is the American phrase? — all about
Robin Hood's barn — but the image said we must follow the
footsteps of Buddha, and so we went on. Old Buddha must have
had a little something to drink, the way his footsteps wandered
around that patch of Asia, cutting hundred-mile circles and
figure-eights in those Cambodian jungles. Perhaps the atmosphere of Cambodia intoxicated him, too.

Pnompenh. If you don't believe it, look on the map. And
those other towns, their pagoda spires and paper lanterns glimmering up suddenly in some recess of the jungle, unexpected,
unreal, enticing as the coloured pictures in the quick-turned
pages of a story-book. Put a rakish-hatted, slog-footed Légionnaire in a fairy tale — afoot in a land of sugar and spice with
buildings made of candy; lakes of *cointreau,* all flavors; forests
of flowers under skies of curly cloud and blue and gold — and
you have an idea of what I was like, going hand in hand with
that beautiful Asian woman to those impossible places at the
instruction of a wooden doll.

But do you wonder I walked like one enchanted? Every
sundown I could ask two questions of that image, and it would
answer me — answer me, I tell you! — in a pixie voice! — in
Parisian French! — moving its lips of wood against my ear! —
sending me to places that couldn't be (and always were) there!
— on my way to the biggest buried treasure in the East. And that
lovely priestess at my side; for all the world, the spirit of a rainbow in her diaphanous sarong; soothing me with her quaintly-
accented talk, quieting my impatience, bidding me put my faith

in our other-worldly guide — that woman who walked beside me, the Goddess of Truth in her arms! *Oui*, it was country of enchantments. If a butterfly had alighted on my wrist and spoken to me in the basso tones of a brother, I would not have been surprised.

The war in Europe? The war in Europe seemed a long ways off from the jungled interior of Cambodia where the orchid's perfume shut out the memory of gunpowder, and the peaceful forest stillness could tame a nature so rapacious as the saladang's and keep him snoozing on his mudbank while we tiptoed by.

My trusted mission to Hanoi? I thought of that at first, *pour sûr*, but that was early in the pilgrimage when I would say to myself, "I still have twenty-four days!" or, "I will find the treasure first, and then deliver the message!" or, "Of course I will start tomorrow, there are eighteen days left to go in."

"We must hurry!" I would blurt at my companion. "Name of a Name! are we never coming to the hiding place of the treasure?"

"Patience," her answer would come with a softness that laid cool fingers on my eyelids. "The treasure of Thibong Linh is not easily found."

"And will it be worth all this travelling when we get there?"

"I am only the priestess, Thera, and I cannot tell you. If you would know the treasure's value inquire of Thibong Linh."

Was a million dollars in gold and precious stones worth looking for? Thibong Linh reported the vault to hold all of that, and the thought of such a fortune seized my brain like a drug. Today I am ashamed of the way I went after that treasure. My lust to get my paws on it overrode my awe of the presence of a great mystery. My fingers itched and my tongue poked out. A gloomy commentary on the mind of man, not so? That my main concern with the Goddess of Truth should be the quickest way to riches! My only excuse is that I was a French Légionnaire who had been living on a penny a day. There are people who should know better who are trying to get into heaven because they think the streets up there are gold.

Non, I thought of nothing but the riches I should stuff my pockets with, and the promised bonanza blinded me to almost everything else. Almost. The sun, itself, could not have blinded me to the beauty at my side, but I became accustomed to her there as one becomes accustomed to dawn and nightfall and takes their priceless splendors for granted. Whoever looks at the stars anymore? We are spendthrift with them because they are always there, and so we ignore them as if they were bits of tinsel. Let them be missing for a week, and there would be a panic that would make our stockmarket riots seem like kindergarten flurries in comparison.

Alors, we travelled mostly at night, that woman and I, and I never looked at the stars and not often enough at her. I was too busy mentally fingering a million dollars to consider my companion or even wonder why she was accompanying me on that dreamland tour. She was wonderful company, too. In the thatch-roofed villages through which we passed, she would make the natives bring us anything we wished. She would show the headman the image of Thibong Linh and he would salaam on his wishbone for an hour. On the pink-and-blue rivers that laced through the jungle, she would produce a canoe from practically nowhere, and paddle with me, stroke for stroke, like a man. On the trail, uphill and downhill, her sandals were tireless. And in the daytime, when we slept, she would find some sheltered nook by a stream or pool, make a fire and prepare a little meal of fish and fruit and coconut wine. *Dieu!* I will never forget those days with her in the jungle. How I would roll up and fall asleep on a bed of ferns, and wake up to find her scraping the mud from my boots, sewing a rent in my ragged tunic, or repairing a dent in the leather visor of my *képi.*

"You have slept well, Monsieur Légionnaire? The sun has been down an hour, and it is time to go. I have asked Thibong Linh if we are near the treasure, and she reminds us to have patience — Lu-ong Kuampur is not far. But she says there are dangers, and we must hurry on."

Now throughout all that journey we were followed, you understand, and that is why we travelled at night. I knew that rat-pack from Saïgon was after us, because sometimes in the gloomy stillness I could hear them coming. The woman told me they were after the image, and it didn't take any imagination for me to understand why. So our amazing journey across Cambodia was in reality a continual flight, and that night it seemed to me my companion was very worried. All at once it broke through my blindness that for the past week she had been hiding a great anxiety. Fear filled me. Fear of something I had not thought of before.

"Sac à papier!" I reproached myself. "I have been one pig! Look, *mademoiselle!* With that image in your possession your life is not worth a centime. I cannot let you go on like this — ! *Mon Dieu* — !"

"But where else can I go?" she whispered sadly.

"You must hide! Stay in some convent! Something! We must find a place — !"

"And you do not wish to find the goddess's treasure — ?"

"Give Thibong Linh to me!" I babbled. "I will follow the trail alone. There is no need for you to risk your life in this jungle as — "

"I must go with you," she refused my suggestion. "The image was placed in my care, and I could not surrender her to you, although I know you would bring her back. I must go with you, Monsieur Légionnaire, for in helping you find the treasure, Thibong Linh and I will repay the risk you took for us."

Well, I wanted to find that treasure vault, and so we went on. The image sent us to Binh Dinh. From there we went to Quang Gai. We had to keep a move on, *messieurs.* That Saïgon batch never let up chasing us for a minute, and Thibong Linh told me we must not slow down. We moved like a family of Gypsies, the three of us — a woman, a wooden image, a ragged Légionnaire — about the strangest family of Gypsies to ever take the trail. Those yellow devils from Saïgon followed us too closely. I had snatched a hunting knife from a Laos beggar we had met along the trail, and one night I told the woman to go ahead, and I lay in wait for the pursuit. Sure enough. It was not long before I heard the *plut-plut-plut* of bare feet coming along the jungle's floor, and presently one of those hairy Saïgon river rats, the advance scout of the party after us, came nosing along our tracks.

He jumped on me with a yell, and I cut him to pieces and left him there with his knife in his chest as a warning to the others to keep their distance. But at Quang Gai they were so close I could almost feel them breathing on my neck. The fear in my companion's beautiful eyes was constant. As we ran through the palm groves she would turn pale and look back. I did not like that a little bit. I wanted to stop and fight them, but the woman said no, we must not stop, not if we ever wanted to reach the treasure.

Mention of the treasure was all that was necessary to keep me going full steam ahead. Then the image talked in my ear and said we did not now have far to go, and that information drove me as before a bullwhip. I wanted to find that bonanza before those rats on our heels caught up with us and asked for a share. I wanted to pocket the treasure, and then hide the woman and her precious relic somewhere where she would be safe. We left Quang Gai at once, at the advice of the image. Moving under forced draught, we circled into the hills beyond Moulapoumak.

And there another worry attached itself to my heels. Something that harried me a whole lot more than a batch of Cambodian cut-throats from Saïgon. A fear that hit me from the back of my head like a bullet out of ambush. Listen —

Away back near Pnompenh we had passed some Legion patrols. My special permit had let us through, and I had laughed at those sun-bitten soldiers slogging along in the sweat and dust. Do you see? I had laughed myself sick at them, and made up my mind, without realizing it, that I would never go back to them. Since then I had not thought of them. Long ago I had forgotten about the message to Hanoi.

And in those tinted hills beyond Moulapoumak I got a jolt. We were camped for the day in a jasmine grove by an amethyst lake; with Thibong Lingh in her arms the beautiful woman was asleep. Me, I could not sleep. I had a feeling that those Cambodian trackers might stretch their legs some afternoon while we rested, and come up with us. *Morbleu!* I was not afraid of those yellow mongrels, but on the edge of finding the treasure I did not want to be caught napping. That afternoon I decided to play the little ambush trick on them again, so while the woman slept in the ferns I crept back down the trail the way we had come, thinking to surprise any scouts. There were some scouts in those hills, all right! I saw them on the distant slope of a lavender valley, threshing the ripe undergrowth, this way, that way, as if they were looking for somebody. Like an animal watching hunters, I crouched on a ledge above the valley, amused because they were making little progress.

And then I did not grin. My mouth screwed up as if filled with lemon pie, my eyeballs swelled in terror. About a quarter mile off, that party was, moving slowly through the undergrowth, aimlessly as berry-pickers, scouting the slope in the other direction. But it seemed to me as if they were coming straight at me with the speed of antelopes. They were not that cut-throat gang from Saïgon! Bones of the Little Corsican! *Non!* But the glint of sunlight on rifle barrels. The glimmer of buckles on polished straps. White square-visored caps grouped in consultation. That unmistakable canvas tunic; that famous *képi!*

I was suddenly reminded that the arm of France is long. I was suddenly remembering how the Foreign Legion is everywhere. The dispatch to Hanoi! But in that story-book junket across Wonderland I had lost all count of time — thirty days must have gone by long ago! Holy Saint Catherine! there was a war going on! I had failed to carry out a *mission extraordinaire!* I was a deserter from the French Foreign Legion! The secret service, the army, the Foreign Legion — all the bloodhounds of France would be after me! And the penalty for desertion from the Legion in wartime is death!

That glimpse of those Légionnaires paralyzed me. Going

south, they passed out of sight, but the chance that they might come across my hobnailed track and raise their eyebrows at it made my blood run cold. As sure as sundown the arm of France would reach out for me. I was crazed with fear.

Not of dying — it was to be avoided, not feared. But I did not want to miss my chance at Asia's biggest treasure, and along with that I had been having a good time. How wonderful seemed this wandering across Cambodia, now it might be interrupted. How delightful the tropical evening, the forest hush, the fragrant air. I looked around and saw flowers I had never seen. The sky above the valley was striped with pale greens merging into a sea of burgundy where the western sun-shafts, violet and gold, were spread out like a Japanese fan. Little parrots quarrelled cheerfully in a nearby thicket. Somewhere far off a temple bell tinkled.

Cursing, I fled back to our hiding place. Even as I damned the scouts I had seen, my jawbone rattled at the knowledge that the Legion would soon be looking for me. That night in the Moulapoumak hills I asked our miraculous instructress a different sort of question.

Panting into our hide-out, I saw my companion had done something she had never done before. Always, save for the few moments when she surrendered it to my hands, the woman had kept the image in her clasp; sleeping or waking, it was by her side. That evening she had left it on the shore, and gone into the amethyst lake for a swim. *Dieu!* she was something to look at out there in the water. Beautiful? A pale Chinese moon hung over the jungle tops, and the woman was like a naiad among the lilies. Her luminous form took my breath away as she saw me and rested her cheek against the water and started swimming for shore.

Figure to yourself the panic I was in when I tell you I turned my back on her. *Oui,* I turned my back on that vision and grabbed up the little image; tore loose the silk coverings, and held the carved wooden face against my ear. I had to ask my question in a hurry. You bet I did.

"Will the Legion ever capture me?"

My voice was a harsh, low rattle in my throat, for the woman was nearing the bank, and I did not want her to know about that desertion business. The answer came in a whisper, too; I had to press the fluttering lips against my ear to catch the faint, squeaky reply.

"No one will overtake you if you proceed more swiftly than they. Have courage. Keep east on the trail and tonight you will reach Lu-ong Kuampur where the treasure is hidden. The Vault of the Stored Moonbeams is only a kilometer from here."

Never had the wooden lips spoken at such length, and never such a message. Only a kilometer! I shouted out loud. I held the Goddess of Truth in front of me and made as if to kiss her, but cool, wet hands reached around my elbow and took her from me. Dripping, turquoise garden statue in her translucent silk sarong, the woman was there. Hugging Thibong Linh to her bosom, she regarded me with widened eyes.

"You are frightened tonight, Monsieur Légionnaire. You have seen something off in the jungle. What did you ask of Thibong Linh?"

"Only a kilometer! Lu-ong Kuampur is only a kilometer — !"

Soberly her deep eyes looked into mine, looked through my excitement to my anxiety. "I know," she whispered softly. "Come! We must fly — "

Her sandals were as wings flitting off up the moon-surfaced trail, and I was after her at the strain of every leg muscle. The Goddess of Truth had said something when she told me that treasure was only a kilometer distant, and she had said something else about no one overtaking me if I proceeded more swiftly than they. But there was a catch in that last bit of honesty. How fast were my enemies proceeding? I took no chances with that, and as I went at full stride I kept a watch over my shoulder and was ready for rearguard action with drawn knife.

The woman, the little image and I, we went like the wind. Three faces East! It was one of those bright nights, all black and yellow and silver, the sort of night when the Little People hold their dances in the grass. The moon cast a sharp-edged shadow. One should take care, in Asian moonlight as bright as that.

Our trail led into a forest of sandalwood that looked drugged. There was a smell of cloves. Sinbad might have landed somewhere around there on his magic carpet. Aladdin got the oil from those sleeping tropic flowers for his wonderful lamp. That forest in Indo-China was steeped in mystery. What? Consider a Legion deserter chasing after a priestess named Thera, who carried at her bosom a goddess of wood that could talk. *Voila!* Exactly at what I judged to be a kilometer from where we had started, the woman swerved off the trail into a clump of poincianas, pushed aside the blossoms, gave a little cry of awe as she pointed to a doorway in the ground.

Do you know what it resembled, that doorway screened by flowers? Entrance camouflaged, steps going down, it looked like the entrance to one of those concrete dugouts you can see today in the Maginot Line, one of those armored subways under the fortified French frontier. Only the stones of those down-going steps were a whole lot older than any modern architecture. Those steps were so old they looked like grey sponge, and they climbed down into a darkness that hurt my eyes. That stairwell went deep. Father Time lived down there. I could smell his breath as I peered down those deep-descending steps. *Zut!* His breath was not good.

The woman pointed at some characters chiselled in the stone casement. "The Vault of the Stored Moonbeams, Monsieur Légionnaire. Wait — "

I was paused on the lowest moon-lit step when she said that, trembling, hardly able to restrain my legs. She slipped off into the camouflage a moment, returning with a lighted flambeau. I do not know where she found that oily torch-wood, or how she lighted it. Perhaps by a moon-ray. She was a remarkable woman.

Side by side we crept down the steps, the woman holding the torch and clutching Thibong Linh, me holding my breath and clutching my knife. We were like two children starting down the stairs late at night to see the Christmas tree. Awed. In excitement. Unable to wait. And a little scared.

And a little more scared as the steps went farther down. Suppose there wasn't any Santa Claus? And scared a little more as the steps went down farther. What was that peculiar smell? Father Time had a bad case of halitosis down there. A staggering case. Ancient plaster and damp rot and something else, I could not tell what. The woman caught a whiff of it, and looked at me. Her eyes did not like it, but she thrust the torchlight ahead of her and went on down.

I remember a stone door ajar at the bottom, and how the torchlight went in ahead into blackness, and how that bad breath came out. It was enough to almost quench the torch-flare, but nothing could quench my desire to get in and have a look at the treasure. Certainly nothing like a gust of stale air. I leapt down the three bottom steps, kicked open the door. But then my companion slipped by me and went in first. *Sacré!* past the threshhold we stood rooted. Rooted in that underground vault by a pair of gold eyes!

My faith, they were terrible eyes! Solid gold, lidless, blazing from blackness in a corner like the eyes of a bodyless wizard enraged at our intrusion. It was Father Time. *Non,* someone had eaten up Father Time; his bones were in a bloody pile in mid floor. His bones and little scraps of cloth. His family, too? There were three skulls! I will not describe to you the mess on the floor of that cellar. The woman screamed. The gold eyes from the corner leapt at us like automobile headlights. There was an arched streak of black and orange blurs. One roar, and I was fighting with a tiger!

Now I am going to tell you about something that happened to me. This part of the story I cannot guarantee by explanation; it was an emotional experience — you will have to take my word for it. You know how they saw a drowning man in one second can see his whole past life before him? It was something like that. In the flash when those gold eyes jumped and I saw it was a tiger, it was as if cataracts were peeled from my vision. I saw the

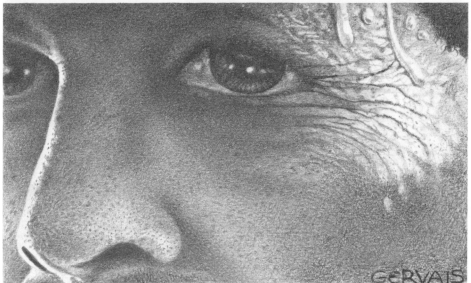

tiger leaping at a girl. I saw the days I had spent with her in the flowered jungle. I saw her swimming in an amethyst lake; her face as I had seen it in moonlight; her graceful walk at my side; her gentle hands sewing my torn tunic; her cool smile; her eyes —

I do not know how I flung myself in front of that girl. I would have thrown myself in front of an express train for her, *oui*, and I would have beaten it, too. That tiger hit me like a blast from the muzzle of a cannon. With the roar of a howitzer. With the impact of a zooming airplane. I can show you the marks of that collision. I went down like a straw bag under a rushing charge of steel bayonets, but I could never show you how I fought back. With a tiger. Ravening. On that greasy floor. Lights and shadows flying. Snapping and roars. Myself on that wild brute's back (before God, I do not know how!) my left arm locked about his throat, right fist flailing the knife. Do you imagine what it would be like to have an arm around a volcano of orange and black flame? To wrestle with an explosion? To roll, bound and twist with one lightning-muscled Gorgon of solid violence? *Messieurs,* the memory of those giant snapping jaws sends a river of shivers down my spine. The great sickle-clawed paws slashing air. The terrible, kicking hind legs. If those hind feet had come up under me they would have scooped me out like a cantaloupe. One bat from a forepaw would have killed me. Looking back, he could have bitten off my head. I saw down his throat in that instant when he struck me. His fangs were bared scimitars, his breath like a million empty salmon cans.

I must have knifed that tiger in the jugular vein first stab, otherwise I do not think I would be here. Probably he was dying when we crashed to the floor, and I was battling his dying reflexes. But the dying reflexes of those Asian jungle cats are like a box of exploding hand grenades. From wall to wall we pitched, locked in dreadful contortion, flopping, tumbling. The roars of the beast shook that underground chamber like an earthquake. Sweat filled my eyes. Fur smothered me. It seemed to last a long, red time. Again and again I struck with the knife. His last scratch got my left arm; ripped my elbow open as if with shrapnel.

Afterwards I discovered three fractured ribs, a shoulder sprain, the skin scraped off one leg from knee to thigh. Only a fury which matched the tiger's had saved me. The power which charged through me in that flash when the beast sprang at the girl. *Non*, I did not feel my picayune injuries when I reeled to my feet. And that was a big tiger. Almost seven feet long, stretched out on the floor amidst the left-overs of last night's supper. I did not look at that.

I looked at the girl in the doorway of that Vault of Stored Moonbeams. She was crying. Not in terror with her face askew, but differently. Silently. Standing there on the threshhold, torch upheld, chin lifted — she had not run, *messieurs!* She was looking at me marble-pale, her eyes as stars with tears.

"You save my life, Monsieur Légionnaire. Again! That tiger — "

I nodded foolishly.

"But there is nothing," her low voice broke on a sob. "The vault — the vault is empty. There is nothing here but those men who were here before us — and that tiger. There is no treasure—"

"Why, but there is!" I can see myself charging at her, waving my arms like a blockhead. "I have found my treasure, *mademoiselle*. All the treasure I ever want, and I had to come all this way to find it! Do you see? Do you see?" I was rushing her up the steps to get her out of that evil den. Yelling as I carried her up into the sweet air and moonlight to set her down among the fragrance of poincianas.

And then I give you my word, I could not speak to her. *Non!* I had killed a tiger — I could have killed another — but facing so much beauty in the moonlight, I could not get out the question I wanted to ask. "Thibong Linh!" I whispered, thick-tongued. "Give me Thibong Linh."

Wordless, she handed me the little figure. Will you believe I had to turn my face away to ask my question. What? But all men are fools.

"Does she love me?" My hand was shaking in anxiety as I

held the wooden image-face against my ear. "Does she love me, too?"

It was funny how the wooden lips fluttered. Stammering at my ear, they did not seem able to speak. When the answer, the one word came, it seemed as if Thibong Linh was choking in emotion, too.

"*Chérie!*" I shouted, whirling, clasping her in my arms, dizzy. "Beautiful! Wonderful! We will marry at once! Tomorrow! Ah, sacred girl! We will spend the rest of our days in these flowered forests! What? *Non*, do not be sad! We will spend our days in these forests together, and live a thousand years!" With Thibong Linh between us, I hugged her and danced.

So she kissed me, that girl. Once! And for everything in my life I was repaid. For the dreary misfortune that sent me in exile from Paris. For the kicks and batterings of luck that have knocked me around the globe. For the disappointments, the shin-bangs, the stupidities, the failures. *Oui*, even for the hobnailed boots that came crashing through the poinciana shrubs that night, the sweaty grinning faces, the hard-jawed Legion captain who rushed at me out of nowhere, his voice like gunfire blasting away a dream.

"Nice work, Corday! Take the woman, boys! Sergeant, just duck down into that hole and see if there are any more of her crowd below. March along with the dancer, lads, and lock her in that stone hut near the camp. Did you know our tents were just over the hill, Corday? *Mon Dieu!* and we have been trying to find this very dugout for weeks. Tonight we thought we heard a tiger. But they wired from Quang Gai you were headed this way. Why, man, you look just like hell!"

He stopped his rapid-fire shouting to stare. Then he wheeled, bawling at the Légionnaires. "Well, what are you standing like sticks for, you fools! Get that woman into the guard house, double quick. *Allons!*"

CHAPTER IV

I leave it to you, my feelings when I saw those soldiers form a cordon around that flower-faced girl. Right oblique! Forward March! Tramp, Tramp, Tramp. In a little brown cloud of moon-dust they swung by, and I stood too stunned for protest or belief.

Just as the squad clicked by, the girl reached out and thrust a silken bundle into my hands. I saw her eyes were shining with tears. "Take it, *mon brave*. A little souvenir to remember me by. And remember, too, that she did tell the truth. About the two greatest things in the world. And at the last."

With that she was gone in the moonlight, and I found myself with Thibong Linh in my hands. I remember the sergeant coming up the dugout steps, howling something about wireless instruments, some bones, a dead tiger. I remember screaming, "Wait! She has done nothing, you fools! Wait!" and fighting the Legion captain and the sergeant all the way through the sandal-woods to a camp. Men were bivouacked in a barbwire clearing, and I was dragged to an officer's tent. The captain flung me into a camp chair; stood over me with a Red Cross kit, bellowing and grinning.

"Don't be an idiot, my boy! No, but I cannot blame you, you are not the first to fall in love with that siren. Hold on — let me bandage that — maniac! — I am offering congratulations. You will win the *Croix de Guerre*, the *Medaille Militaire* — for your part in helping capture the greatest spy in the East — "

"It is a mistake!" I howled. "She is never a spy! She is the priestess, Thera, from the Temple of the Moon in Angkor Wat. She was trying to save the goddess, Thibong Linh — from a gang of yellow thugs, the night I left Saïgon headquarters. They

185

were fighting her in an alley off Rue Catinat — trying to steal from her the Goddess of Truth — "

"Priestess Thera! Goddess of Truth, be damned!" he gave me saltily. "That woman is a German-paid spy, Corday, their most dangerous agent in Asia. Headquarters sent you out for her as bait!"

"Bait!" I whispered.

"And do you think they would start a Légionnaire walking across Indo-China, alone, inexperienced in dispatch work, with an important military message like that? You were bait, *mon gar,* and they took you hook, line and sinker. The German agents. We knew there must be spies there in Saïgon Headquarters — they relayed your departure to their chief. Their chief was that woman, Corday. Of course. That alley fight was staged for you, a snare of their own manufacture. They were not certain if you had an important message, and they dared not kill you without finding out what it was. But our agents caught them in their own trap. Throughout that alley chase, throughout your trip across Cambodia, the French Secret Service and a Legion detachment were following you. Pardon me, but I have been in constant touch with the Intelligence Department, and I know. All that priestess business of hers, that chase through the jungle was a trick to draw you along. Those were her own men following you; they must have discovered our men trailing them, and signalled her something was wrong. Doubtless she kept you with her because she was unable to find your hidden secret. Why she brought you to that dugout wireless station, I can only guess. Have you tortured, perhaps. But it seems a tiger cleaned up the place before she got there. *Alors,"* he gestured sympathy, seeing my face, "it is too bad we could not have let you know that she was a fraud."

"Ha, ha!" I screamed. "So Thera was a fraud, was she? Pardon me, Monsieur Captain, but right now I will give you and the smart French Secret Service the surprise of your life!"

He must have had the surprise of his life, all right, when I unwrapped that image from its silk swaddlings, and held its little face to my ear. He must have thought me mad when I asked it to tell me if the woman I loved was a spy or not. "Answer me, Thibong Linh!" I prayed. "Answer loud enough for both of us to hear!"

Can you see me standing there with that wooden goddess to my head? The captain leaning across his camp table with enlarged eyes? Both of us listening, listening for a carved wooden image to speak? *Ah, mon Dieu!* The wonderful lips of Thibong Linh! Those lips moved, *messieurs!* Those wooden lips moved against my ear. That captain saw them moving, too. But no voice came!

I clutched the image desperately, and shouted for it to speak. The lips continued moving, but no voice came out. *Non,* it was voiceless, dumb. I must have hurled it to the floor as one hurls a suddenly dislocated telephone, for I heard the crash, and there was the image in pieces at my feet. And like an instrument, too, there also was its mechanism.

The head was broken off, and we could see the lips in that face still moving, opening and shutting on an inner hinge, operated on the sort of bobbin that moves the eyes of a doll. Like a doll the image was hollow, and there were wooden cog-wheels inside it. Also a little rubber bulb that could be inflated or squeezed by a lever concealed in the image's bottom.

In a flash that Legion *commandant* seemed to understand. He understood, also, that my own insides had broken up in that smash.

"The Asians are clever at making that sort of toy," he said kindly, pushing me into a chair and pressing a cognac bottle into my hand. "It is too bad, *mon gar,* but at least you will have more satisfaction for the double-crossed affections than most men. Tonight she lets down her hair in the guard house, and at dawn you will hear a little echo from the firing squad."

Presently, sorting some papers behind his desk, he looked up over his glasses.

"It might interest you to know. Her name is Margaret Zelle. A Dutch exile from Java. Exotic dancer — courtesan entertainer.

Called herself a Javanese name that means 'Eye of the Morning.'" The *commandant* snorted. "How do you like that? Female spy who calls herself an eye! Of the morning, certainly. Of the evening, too, you can count on it."

I closed my eyes and groaned. "I swear she asked no questions about my mission."

"No need, with those cigars she gave you. Look." The captain produced one of those black cheroots. "We found this among her effects in her Saïgon hotel room. The outer leaves," he peeled off some of the cigar " — these are tobacco. But the inner core? Solid marijuana — the brain-melting IndoChina kind — interwoven with hashish. And that liquor she fed you! Enough to send a rhinocerous to dreamland. You were doped, Corday. Drugged to the eyeballs. And while you slept the Eye doubtless searched you from head to foot."

But I did recall her hands on me in the night as I dreamed beside her. Searching, of course. And those times she mended my tunic and sewed the lining in my *kepi.* Going over me with a comb.

Again I groaned.

"Do not worry," the captain said. "You are not the first victim she hoodwinked. Our intelligence reports name a couple of princes, a Belgian diplomat, a Russian grandee, officials by the dozen. Listen. Our government has censored the fact, but this lady wormed her way into the graces of General Messimy, head of France's War Department. Ha! She shared a Paris love nest with him on the eve of the war." He raised his eyes to the ceiling. "I wish someone would tell me why high-ranking officers and government bigwigs spend so much time spilling war plans in the boudoirs of such women." He frowned at me. "I would expect it of a general, but not of a veteran Légionnaire."

How could I tell him she got nothing from me? That message he had ordered me to carry was in code. And only seven words. *Alors,* I had memorized them at the outset. Which had seemed very lucky, for I lost that secret paper in our flight through that catacomb tunnel under Saïgon.

But it was no consolation to learn the whole affair with that woman had been nothing but hallucinary drugging. That it was fakery from start to finish with that lying Truth Fairy! That talking image. Its ear-kissing lips and pixie voice. All that had been auto-suggestion — the *commandant's* word for it — along with drugged hallucination.

The captain shook his head. "Do not feel too badly, Corday. Not every soldier of the Legion gets a chance to spend a few nights with an Eye of the Morning. She will go down in history as this war's wickedest but most alluring spy. I doubt if even General Messimy won all the attention you did from — to call your priestess by her Javanese name — Mata Hari. . . . "

EPILOGUE

Old Thibaut Corday wrinkled his beard with a sigh, and slumped back deflatedly in his chair, leaving the name of Germany's greatest World War spy in the tobacco smoke before us as casually as if it were the gilt calling card of a princess tossed on the table.

It was the American who picked it up in astonishment. "Mata Hari! The — the dancer! The actress! *The* Mata Hari — ?"

The old Legion veteran nodded as if it didn't matter. His eyes were sombre.

"But — Mata Hari!" the American repeated, obviously unable to believe the name. "Good Lord! Corday, it couldn't have been. She was a German spy and all that — Asian, too — but she was in France the last year of the War. Sure. Dancing in Paris before the diplomats. Your secret service caught her in Paris and she was executed as a spy somewhere in France."

A faint, admiring twinkle shone darkly in the old veteran's eye. "So I have heard it reported, my friend. But I would hate to bet on that report. I would sooner bet she talked herself out of that prison in France, the way she must have talked herself out of that guard house in Cambodia. You recall how the Légionnaires had her there, waiting to be shot? In the morning when the firing squad called for her she was not there. No door had opened, but just before dawn the sentries had heard her call them a good-bye from some bushes off to the left. When they ran to investigate — gone! When they returned to the guard house — empty! Like that," Old Thibaut Corday snapped his fingers, "she was gone. She talked herself out of that guard house, *messieurs.* She was a wonderful woman, and I would bet she could talk herself out of anything."

"But the image!" the British consular agent cried. "Maybe the woman had conversational powers, but how about that image of Thibong Linh. You said its lips moved by some sort of clock-work — "

"Some very cunning clock-work, *oui!* I think she must have wound it up while she held it in her arms, and when I held it against my ear, you comprehend, my fingers gripped on a button or a spring like the lever that made her smoke."

"But the voice!" was the Englishman's protest. "Really, old man! Cog-wheels might work the wooden lips, but to make an image talk — answer all those questions like that — I mean, a voice — "

"I wondered about it, too," Old Thibaut Corday nodded. "I wondered much. Some sort of gramophone record — but even a Victrola cannot answer questions. Wireless sending? But there were no wires. *Non,* cog-wheels did not solve the voice from those wooden lips. But some years after the War I was on leave in Paris. The Legion had given me a month's furlough, and it was my last night before returning to Algiers to serve out my enlistment."

Old Thibaut Corday paused to stare out at the quiet darkness. "Are you familiar with the Moulin Bleu? It is a little theatre off the Rue Pigalle, what the English call a variety show. I stopped in late, just before the curtain of the final act. That last act was billed as The Wonderful Zelda. That was her name — The Wonderful Zelda. She was swathed in Oriental veils, and sitting in the center of the stage with a glass of water in one hand and a figure on her knee. *Sapristi!* She had it puff on a cigar. Then she asked it questions, and while she drank the glass of water that figure would move its wooden lips and answer her. How the audience roared. 'Tell them the two greatest things in the world, little one.' And the figure replied shrilly, 'Love and peace!' She hugged up the figure, kissed it and ran off the stage. The crowd roared applause, but I Thibaut Corday, did not roar. Do you know what that dummy was? It was the wooden dummy of a Foreign Légionnaire, *messieurs!* A Foreign Légionnaire with a toy uniform and bright blue eyes, a too-big nose and a cinnamon beard — a dummy of *me!*

"I got to the stage door on feet of air, but already she had gone. A very strange performer, the doorman told me. Never gave her real name or where she stayed, and she treated that dummy as if it was her very life. 'Her act closed tonight, and she has gone to play at the Palladium Theatre in London.' London! I ran half the way to the boat train. And then I remembered. I was a soldier of the French Foreign Legion! Ah, *mon Dieu!* I had deserted the Legion once; I could not desert it again."

It was growing dark.

Old Thibaut Corday passed a hand across his eyes, and when he sighed back this time their twinkle had faded. "From Algiers I sent a telegram," and the tone had gone from his voice, "only to learn The Wonderful Zelda had been killed trying to rescue her dummy in that fatal Palladium fire. But a lot of people would have been surprised to learn that wonderful ventriloquist was Mata Hari, the War's greatest spy. Only she was more than a ventriloquist, more than a spy. She gave me the two greatest things in the world," said Old Thibaut Corday huskily. "And only a goddess would have done that for a Légionnaire."

AUTHOR'S POSTSCRIPT

In 1932, when this story was written, it was not known for certain whether the French had indeed executed Margaret Zelle or traded her for some valuable Allied agent and shot some minor *espionne* as a substitute (to satisfy public demand) instead. Attributed to distinguished French journalist Georges du Parcq was the story she was promised a blank-cartridge firing squad before whom she could fake her death. After which, alive in a presumably air-conditioned casket, she would be smuggled into neutral Holland or somewhere.

Why let Mata Hari off? Not only might a substitution save a French spy's life. But the exchange might include embarrassing mash notes penned by her lover, General Messimy, the French War Minister, whose name did not float to the surface until years later, when another cabinet minister was mistakenly accused of the Mata Hari connection, convicted and sentenced, and Messimy confessed after the innocent minister had spent years in exile. Meantime, it became evident late in the 30's that Mata Hari had actually been executed, probably in reprisal for the German shooting (in 1915) of Edith Cavell, Red Cross Nurse Rose-of-No-Man's-Land caught operating as a British secret agent in Belgium. By odd coincidence, Mata Hari, at one point in her spy career, posed as a Red Cross Nurse. Both of these ladies proved a propaganda Nemesis for German General von Bissing, who was later fatally poisoned by a Belgian lady spy. But all this did not emerge from behind secret service and censorship curtains until the late 1930's. At which time it became historically apparent that the war-going female of the species could be as deadly as the male and secret intelligence would do well to concentrate on the old stratagem, *Cherchez la femme.*

T.R.